Pop! The holographic Chris  disappeared in a flash of light and suddenly in its place stood— *Mashela!*

Missy lurched back in surprise and toppled onto her backside.

"Well, hello there, Christmas beauty!" Mashela greeted with a wide smile. She was wearing a frumpy, red Santa Claus suit, complete with a shiny, black belt. Her curly, black hair dangled out from under a bent hat. As Missy's head cleared she realized it wasn't Mashela—but a hologram of her.

"Pardon me for doing a little Robin-Hooding. Just didn't seem right that there are *so* many poor people out there while you *Christians* sit in your warm house and open your expensive presents. I looked and, to tell you the truth, they weren't all that great anyway. Your mother totally missed it on a sweater she bought you. Yellow and orange just aren't your colors."

Mr. Ashton said, "What *is* this?!"

"Daddy," Missy said, rising, "meet Mashela Knavery—my thorn in the flesh."

Mashela continued. "I know what you're thinking. No big deal. You weren't attached to those presents—those *things*. Really? Then just think about your reaction when you found out they were missing. *You* can replace them if you want. Please do. I could use more. Oh and don't even try to beat me. Remember, I'm well-trained and much sneakier than you since I don't have to worry about my 'Christian' convictions." Her brown eyes grew big. "I don't have any."

"Lord, give me wisdom," Missy whispered.

Look for these other books in the *Commander Kellie and the Superkids*ᴛᴍ Series!

Commander Kellie and the Superkids™

#8

The Year Mashela Stole Christmas

Christopher P.N. Maselli

KENNETH
COPELAND
PUBLICATIONS

Based on the characters created by Kellie Copeland Swisher, Win Kutz, Susan Wehlacz and Loren Johnson.

Commander Kellie and the Superkids~TM~

The Year Mashela Stole Christmas

ISBN-10 1-57562-659-4   30-0908
ISBN-13 978-1-57562-659-8

17 16 15 14 13 12   11 10 9 8 7 6

Kenneth Copeland Publications
Fort Worth, TX 76192-0001

For more information about Kenneth Copeland Ministries, visit kcm.org or call 1-800-600-7395 (U.S. only) or +1-817-852-6000.

Dedication

To my family at Cornerstone Faith Center in Sioux City, Iowa, for helping me through many persecutions when I was Missy's age.

And to my persecutors, thanks for the inspiration.

Contents

Hello Superkid,

I'm Missy Ashton and this is my story. (I've always wanted to say that.) But, actually, it's true! This is a story about what I went through during my favorite time of the year: Christmas! I love all the bright lights, friendly smiles and—hold me back—the store sales. Of course, that's not what Christmas is *all* about. Christmas is about loving, giving and celebrating Jesus. That's why when my Christmas was threatened, it really got to me.

Let me back up and fill you in a bit: I'm a Superkid at Superkid Academy. SKA is my training ground not only for academics, but also for becoming the person God created me to be. I've learned *tons* with my friends at SKA—Paul, Rapper, Valerie, Alex and our leader, Commander Kellie. We always have great adventures in God.

Anyway, this story starts at the beginning of what was supposed to be our Christmas vacation. Paul and Rapper came home to my house for the holiday. Little did I know someone *else* decided to tag along…"someone who has made herself an enemy of Superkid Academy…." Someone who has made herself my enemy….

Maybe you've had trouble like this. Maybe someone you know has tried to become your enemy because you believe in God. Maybe they make fun of you, spread lies about you, steal from you or even try to harm you. If you know someone like that, then, friend, lemme tell ya, we're in the *same* boat. I only hope my example—though not perfect—will help you deal with that troublemaker in your life.

Merry Christmas—all year 'round!

Missy

The Year Mashela Stole Christmas

"Yeeeeeoooooowwwwww!!!" the big, animated cat cried, shooting into the air. On the ground, the brown mouse giggled. It's not every day you get to set your enemy's tail on fire.

Uh-oh. Now the cat was plummeting back to earth like a misfired rocket. The mouse cleared out of the way and the cat smashed down, denting the earth beneath him. Still on fire, he ran to a horse trough and jumped in. The water sizzled as the cat wheezed an *"aaaahhhhhhh..."*

"What on *earth* are you watching?!" 13-year-old Missy asked, stopping in her tracks.

From the first row of the in-home theater, Paul and Rapper smiled. Somehow Missy wasn't surprised to find her two friends lounging only 30 minutes into their visit.

"Hey, Missy," Paul said, feathering his blond hair, "would you turn it up?"

Rapper agreed. "Yeaaahhh..."

Missy promptly walked across the back of the room, throwing her long, curly hair out of her blue eyes. She turned the volume down.

"Hey!" the boys said in chorus.

"What *is* this?" Missy demanded.

"This," Paul explained, turning, "is classic American culture. A staple of every child's growing experience."

"It's the 'Zoey and Zuzu Christmas Special,'" Rapper chimed in, still staring at the screen. He grabbed a handful of popcorn and stuffed it into his mouth.

Missy cracked a smile. "You're watching a cat and mouse cartoon? Oh, *please* tell me you guys have something better to do."

Paul's face was blank. "Like what?"

Missy waved a small card. "Like figuring out what to get our Christmas Angel."

Paul's face was still blank.

Looking at the card, Missy said, "We've got a 6-year-old named Chip. His family doesn't have enough money for Christmas, so we're going to buy him some presents. We've already gotten him some clothes, we just need to decide what else to get him. Everyone in Nautical does it. There's a big benefit dinner and everything."

"Missy, we just got here. This is classic American culture. A staple—"

"You don't want to waste your vacation watching cartoons, do you?"

Rapper chimed in again. "I do. Till my dad comes, I

don't wanna think about anything." He stuffed more pop-corn into his mouth.

On screen, Zuzu the mouse was cornered. Zoey licked his chops. *Bing!* A light bulb appeared above Zuzu's head. Without hesitation, he whipped out a can of black paint and painted a hole on the wall. *Zip-zip-zip!* He jumped into it and escaped. When Zoey tried to go after him, his head smashed against the plaster, causing little yellow birds to tweet around his head.

"I don't know how you can watch this," Missy said, still smiling. "It's just cat-and-mouse. The mouse beats the cat, the cat beats the mouse. Episode after episode. No one ever wins. It never changes."

"It's a cartoon."

"But they're catching on fire and running into walls. This helps you relax?"

"Well…yeah, kinda."

"Not me. I'm still reeling from everything that happened with Mashela and this Zooey and Zozo aren't helping."

"Zoey and Zuzu," Rapper pointed out.

Paul said, "Missy, maybe you're a little misguided about this."

Missy dropped her smile. "Misguided?! Paul, don't you remember what Mashela did? First she puts Alex's life on the line for no reason. Then after we capture her, she breaks out and tries to get us at each other's throats by telling us lies. Then she kidnaps Rapper and drops him from who-knows-how-high into a junkyard where he has to face NME villains."

"One," Rapper corrected, holding up one finger, still staring forward. "Just one villain."

"And if that's not enough"—Missy held up her bare, right hand—"she still has the ring you gave me as my covenant brother! Don't get me wrong: I've forgiven her. But lemme tell you, she's caused me a *little bit* of stress. If there's one thing I know—"

Paul raised his hand. Missy stopped. "What?"

"Um, when I said 'misguided,' I meant about the cartoon, not Mashela."

Missy's eyes shifted and she bit her bottom lip. "Oh."

"You are a bit stressed, aren't you?"

Missy nodded. "I guess I am. Yeah."

Rapper laughed. Paul and Missy looked at him. He turned and looked at them. Then he pointed to the screen. "Sorry, I was laughing at them." He stood up. "I'm gonna go get a soft drink." And he left the room.

Paul stood, too, and walked back to Missy. He caught her eye and said, "It's over. We don't know where Mashela is, but it's over for now. In two weeks, when we're back at Superkid Academy, we'll track down Mashela and end this once and for all. But for now…don't think about it. It's your vacation…and it's Christmas."

Missy smiled. She could always count on Paul to cheer her up. "You're right. It's Christmas! I should be having fun! This is my favorite time of year. I'm not going to let anything spoil it. Not even Mashela."

"Now you're talking," Paul said, squeezing her arm. He looked back at the movie screen. "C'mon, join Rapper and me for some Zoey and Zuzu. Maybe this will be the episode where the mouse *finally* drives the cat out of the house. Or maybe the cat will actually *swallow* the mouse. You never know."

"Not likely," Missy said, sitting down. "But if it were… *that's* an episode I'd watch."

▲ ▲ ▲

Though Missy wasn't extremely hungry, dinner didn't come soon enough for Paul and Rapper. Missy's eyes widened when Paul thumped a double helping of sweet potatoes onto his plate. *Where is he going to put that?* she wondered. Sometimes she thought he could eat enough for both of them. Rapper took a little less, but probably, Missy thought, only because he wanted to save room for dessert.

Missy's dad, Gregg Ashton, sat in his usual place: at the foot of the table. He was a tall man with receding, white hair and a cleanshaven face. Bushy, white eyebrows sat above his brown eyes making his nose appear a little smaller than it actually was.

Lois Ashton, Missy's mom, sat catty-cornered to him, as usual, and next to Missy. She was—by anyone's terms—a striking woman, with soft facial features, curly blond hair and blue eyes. Sometimes Missy got tired of the "are you two sisters?" jokes…but, then again, Missy was looking more and more like her mother every day. And Missy liked that.

Both her parents were lean and in good health. Her father was a sharp businessman with a black-and-white outlook on life. His business ventures made him quite wealthy—and everyone knew it since he owned half the town's businesses. He was also very giving, kind and polite, and his faith was strong. Anyone who knew him knew he believed every successful idea he'd had came from the Lord.

Mrs. Ashton was also quite the "people-person." Strong in faith as well, when she wasn't consulting businesses, she worked with organizations to feed the poor, help the jobless or benefit some other portion of society. She was one of the key players in Nautical's Christmas Angel campaign, which is why Missy was used to helping a Christmas Angel every year.

Rapper and Paul sat together, across the table. Rapper was opposite Missy, Paul opposite her mother. Missy was glad they could both join her for Christmas vacation. Rapper was only staying a few days—until December 23, when his dad was coming to pick him up. He was nearly 13 and a friend Missy could count on. She'd only met him a few years ago when she became a Superkid. Truly, they didn't have much in common, but they got along well. Missy didn't know all the details, but she knew Rapper'd had a tough childhood.

Brown-eyed and brown-haired, Rapper was called "Rapper" because he loved to rap, and he always rapped when he was nervous. From what Missy knew, his parents had divorced when he was really young. So holiday after holiday, he went to see one parent or the other, which was hard for him. His mom was a Christian, but his dad wasn't really interested. During Superkid Academy prayer meetings, Rapper always prayed that his father would one day see the light in his son's life.

And then there was Paul. Having grown up an orphan,

he'd never known his parents. Missy had gotten to know Paul more than ever when, a few months ago, Paul had found a clue about his parents. He'd set out to discover more about them and Missy joined him. Their search sent them throughout Missy's hometown of Nautical, and they'd stayed here at her house. In the end, even though he eventually found out his parents were no longer alive, he discovered they had loved him very much. And Missy's parents took it upon themselves to take Paul in as their covenant son. As far as they were concerned, they would be Paul's parents as long as he would let them. That's part of what made this Christmas so special. It was the first Christmas Paul had ever had with a group of people he could call his family. Missy was pleased to call him her brother in the Lord. To Missy, it was a tie even stronger than flesh and blood.

"Earth to Missy, Earth to Missy, *chhhh!*"

Missy blinked and looked at Paul. He was talking into his ComWatch—a communications watch all the Superkids wore so they could talk with each other over short distances. Missy looked down at her own ComWatch. Paul's brown eyes smiled back at her.

"Come in, Missy," he said.

Missy quietly laughed and ended the transmission.

"Sorry," she said, "guess I took off there for a moment."

Paul chuckled. "Your mom asked you a question."

Missy turned to her mom. "Sorry."

"Well, Tootle, I was saying—"

"Tootle?" Rapper questioned.

Missy's mom smiled. "We call her that because—"

Missy grabbed her mother's elbow. "Rapper, you don't want to know."

"Inquiring minds want to know."

Paul shook his head. "Believe me, you don't want to know."

"You know?" Rapper asked.

"Found out last time I was here—and I'm sworn to secrecy," Paul added, shoving some sweet potatoes in his mouth.

Rapper had a big smile on his face. He turned to Missy, "C'mon, tell me. I'm the only one here who doesn't know."

Missy shot him a toothy smile and then turned to her mother. "So what is it you were saying, Mommy?"

"I was saying we call you Tootle because—"

"No!" Missy cried. "Before that! What were you saying *before* that?"

"Oh!" Missy's mother smiled. She lifted up a small, green and red envelope. "I was saying that this came in the mail a few weeks ago. I saved it for you."

Missy stopped eating and took the envelope. She used her butter knife to slice it open. She pulled out an elegant invitation and read it.

"You should enter!" Missy's mom exclaimed.

"What is it, Tootle?" Rapper asked.

Missy shot him a glare. He smiled big and went back to eating.

"It's the Miss Nautical Christmas Pageant," Missy stated, reading over the sheet. She squinted. "I don't know," she said. "I really want to rest this Christmas. These things are just about makeup and hairspray anyway."

"It's up to you, but the grand prize is—"

"—a pretty good chunk of change," Mr. Ashton finished.

"I don't think so," Missy said, putting the invitation back in the envelope and setting it beside her plate. "The practice session is only two days away. There's no time to get ready."

"Oh, you don't need time to get ready," Mrs. Ashton stated. "You're always ready."

"Thanks. But it's on the same night as the Christmas Angel dinner, so…"

"Actually, it's *before* the benefit," Mr. Ashton said. "We have time for both if you want to do it."

Missy looked at Paul. He just smiled.

"No, I need to rest," she said. "But thanks for letting me know about it."

▲　▲　▲

Turning on the Christmas tree was a tradition in the Ashton household—one which the whole family attended. Therefore, after dinner, Mr. and Mrs. Ashton, Missy, Paul and Rapper all retired to the living room. Missy's mother had the whole house decorated in reds and greens—with holly, greenery, crystal snowflakes and more. But tonight the decorating would be completed when they lit the Christmas tree together.

Missy, being the youngest Ashton in the household, always had the privilege of lighting the tree. It was one of her favorite Christmas duties. Of course, tearing open presents wasn't all bad either. Her family had one of the popular "holographic trees"—beautiful all season and easy to clean up. Plus, during off-season, you could pull out the "Christmas tree" holofilm and replace it with, for instance, a "Fireworks" holofilm—Mr. Ashton's personal favorite. Right now, there was no tree in the room at all, just a small, green, oval disc amid a heap of presents.

With Paul and Rapper lounging on the floor and her

parents sitting next to one another on a plush loveseat, Missy reached down through a barricade of presents and pushed a button on the green disc.

Bzzzt! With a slight flicker, the 10-foot holo-tree lit up, filling the corner of the room. Everyone gasped as the beautiful tree appeared, covered in elegant, golden decorations and sparkling, white lights.

"Awesome," Rapper said.

"I programmed it myself," Missy's mother said.

Missy added, "It's beautiful, Mommy." And she walked over and kissed her on the cheek before taking a chair.

For a long moment, everyone sat in silence, staring at the twinkling tree. Christmas was coming and somehow, this set the feeling in stone. The tree was so heartwarming, so encouraging. All the troubles Missy had faced only a few weeks ago were gone now. She could rest in the peace and comfort of Christmas. She could rest, reflecting on the many ways the Lord was good to her.

Missy looked over at the miniature, pearl-colored Nativity scene on a side table. It sparked a feeling inside her, too, like a warm fire on a winter's night. As long as she could remember, her family had owned that Nativity scene, and they displayed it every Christmas next to the tree. The manger and the figures were carved from smooth, milky marble. Each piece stood on its own—Joseph, Mary, the cows, the wise men, the kings, the sheep and goats. She liked to pick them up once in a while because they were always heavier than they looked.

Then her gaze drifted to the window. Outside, a light snow was falling, the sparkling snowflakes reflecting the light from inside the house. *Christmas,* Missy thought, *is the **best** time of year.*

Mrs. Ashton shivered and her husband broke the silence. "Cold? I can get you a blanket."

Missy's mom shook her head and snuggled closer to him. "Just a chill," she said. "I'm not really cold." She looked behind her, out the window. "I don't know what it was."

Gregg Ashton smiled and his eyes lit up. "I should have our guys sew you a fluffy Santa outfit—that would keep you warm. How'd that be for a new clothing line at Ashton Clothiers? Santa outfits?" Mr. Ashton chuckled. He owned Ashton Clothiers, one of the city's most successful businesses.

"I'd buy one if I were a farmer," Paul said.

Missy couldn't help but ask. "And why would you need a Santa outfit if you were a farmer?"

"Because I'd be hoe-hoe-hoeing all day."

Missy let out an exasperated yelp, slapping her hands on her knees. "Ugh! I can't believe I fell for that!"

Rapper tilted his head. "Well, I can tell you, no one in the church that I grew up in would buy one. They don't like anything to do with Santa. You know, some people say stuff like you can rearrange the letters in SANTA and it's SATAN."

Mr. Ashton's white eyebrows bobbed up and down. "Right. And you rearrange the letters in GOD and you get DOG. What's that tell you? Just that the English language is a funny thing."

Rapper chuckled this time. "That *is* funny."

"Actually," Mr. Ashton said, "I've always liked the story of Santa—that is, the original Saint Nick."

"How's that?"

"Well, St. Nicholas was quite a man after God's own heart. The historical facts surrounding him are a bit jumbled—it was so long ago. But there are some stories that are quite interesting."

Mr. Ashton leaned forward.

"They say Nicholas' parents were Christians and prayed for a child. And, lo and behold, soon Nicholas was born. His parents said he was a true gift from God. They raised him to live for God and give gifts to the poor. This is about…what? 280 A.D.?"

Mrs. Ashton nodded.

"About 280 A.D. When Nick was a teenager—about your age—his parents died. But he never stopped living for Jesus. He even became a priest in the church when he was only 19."

"Cool," Paul said.

"Soon he became a bishop. He was quite the leader. His uncle even prophesied over Nicholas, saying he would help many people. Some people say St. Nick would spend all night studying God's Word so he could bring it to the people. He was known for his faith."

Mr. Ashton scratched his jaw. "It's been said that one time, he was caught giving money to a poor family. But Nicholas made the man who caught him promise to keep it a secret. He wanted everyone to give thanks to God for the gifts.

"That's why," Mr. Ashton said, pointing his finger, "as far as I'm concerned, the true St. Nicholas is a picture of what Christmas is all about. His life is an example of living for God and giving. Of course, God wants us to be givers. He's the greatest Giver of all—He gave us His Son Jesus, and we celebrate that Gift now and all year 'round."

Paul said, "Sounds like you've told that story before."

Mr. Ashton leaned back. "Does it sound rehearsed? Well, I guess I heard that story time and again when I was Toot's age."

Missy threw her hands up. "Whoa…OK, Daddy. I draw the line at 'Toot.'"

Mr. Ashton winked at his daughter. "When I was *Missy's* age, my father told me that story whenever I was picked on. Some kids who walked home the same way I did used to throw snowballs at me every winter. No apparent reason. Just to stir me up, I guess. They knew I was a Christian. I wanted to get them back something awful."

"Daddy, that's so sad."

"Well, honey, most of God's people are hit with persecution at one time or another. The devil makes sure of it. But, like St. Nick, we shouldn't seek revenge. We need to keep giving out and not giving in. Galatians 6:9 says, 'Let us not become weary in doing good, for at the proper time we will reap a harvest if we do not give up.'"

"Boy, hold me back," Missy stated. "Don't be beating up on my daddy! What's he ever done to you?" She held up a playful fist.

"Careful, Missy," Paul interjected. "Don't wanna end up with coal in your stocking."

"I'm just saying I wouldn't take it. I've heard about

Christians, you know, who allow others to make fun of them every day and pick on them. Not me. I'd give it right back if I had to."

"They'll know we're Christians by our love," Paul said, referring to John 13:35.

"L! O! V! E!" Missy shouted, punching the air with each letter.

"Oh that's great, Tootle," her mom said flatly. "That'll win 'em over."

Missy put her hands back in her lap and grinned. "I'm just *joking*," she said. "I'd stick to the Word."

"That's the real challenge," Rapper said. "I mean, I've been in plenty of fights, given my background." He looked at Missy's parents and added, "Before I was a Christian, I was in a gang. Really bad deal." Then he continued, "And as a Christian, I believe in standing up for yourself. You know, if someone tries to hurt you, you can defend yourself. But sometimes there's a fine line. I'll tell you, when Mashela kidnapped me a couple months ago, it was *easy* to get into that place of wanting to sock it to her—and good."

Paul chimed in, "Movies and television tell you getting revenge is cool as long as the other person deserves it. But in Romans 12:19 the Word states, 'Do not take revenge,' because the Lord says, 'It is mine to avenge; I will repay.'

Truth is, our lives—especially during persecution—can say more than any words we could ever use."

"Check it out," Rapper added. "In Acts 7, Stephen was stoned to death for being a Christian. But he took it rather than fighting back. And his life became a testament to everyone there."

"Even Jesus was persecuted," Mr. Ashton said. "But He didn't fight back or get mouthy. He just used the wisdom God gave Him and His silence ministered more than we'll ever know."

Missy let out a long breath. Memories of her struggle with Mashela came back to her. That girl had twisted things into knots and pushed Missy further than ever. Along the way, Missy had sure let her know what she thought about it. Missy bit her lip. In hindsight, maybe that hadn't been the best strategy. But it had sure helped her blow off steam at the time. She shook her head and let out a long breath. Through it all, she'd found out how important it was not to get offended. Just as she'd discovered then, she knew now, she had to let it go. It was over. And she wasn't going to let the troubles of the past flood her mind during her favorite holiday ever. Paul was right. She had to let it go. She *would* let it go.

Mrs. Ashton must have noticed the look on Missy's

face, because she asked, "Are you all right, Tootle?"

Missy shook it off. "Yeah. Sorry I faded out again. Just thinking about that mess with Mashela."

"I didn't mean to bring her up," Rapper said.

"No—It's OK."

"Well, after the stories you've told us, she sounds like a real menace to me," said Mr. Ashton.

Paul stated the obvious. "She needs Jesus."

Then Rapper added, "Hey—don't let her steal your Christmas."

Missy tilted her head and looked over at Rapper. She winked. "No one can steal Christmas from you," Missy corrected. "Christmas can only be stolen if you *let* it be stolen."

"Amen," Paul said.

Mrs. Ashton shivered again. She turned her head and looked out the window for a moment. Then she snuggled closer to her husband.

▲ ▲ ▲

Through tiny binoculars she watched. And she waited. Her breath lingered in the cold air.

Ever since she'd met Missy, her life had turned upside down. The only friend she'd ever had didn't trust her anymore. And this Miss-Holier-Than-Thou had it perfect in every way. She didn't know how hard life really was. That's why she found it so easy to spit out a Pollyanna "God loves you"—as if she understood the first thing about life, about love.

She pulled down the binoculars and smiled wickedly. Miss-Holier-Than-Thou was about to learn a thing or two.

▲ ▲ ▲

Sitting at a cherry-wood vanity in her room, Missy brushed her hair with a big, wooden brush. She did this every night, without fail. She knew the moment her head hit the pillow, her hair would twist and knot, but that was OK. Such was life. Missy brushed her hair every night because it relaxed her.

Everyone had said their goodnights and Paul and Rapper were more than thrilled to each have their own room. Missy guessed neither one was used to living in the luxury of a big house. OK, *mansion.* That was 30 minutes ago. Since then, Missy had changed into a flannel night-gown, brushed her teeth, gargled with mouthwash and removed her makeup. Now, as was her ritual, she was brushing her hair—the final step before dreamland.

All in all, it had been a great day. The further into the

day, the better, the closer to Christmas. Evergreens, snowmen, sleigh bells. Pageants. Missy stopped brushing and
looked at herself in the mirror. She slid her fingers over a
small "up" arrow on the mirror and it zoomed in 10%,
15%, 20%. Missy let go. She stared into her own soft, blue
eyes. She pulled her hair back and turned her head slightly.
A short breath escaped her lips. She was looking more and
more like her mother.

Brushing a small sparkle from her chin, Missy's eyes
caught a glimmer of gold behind her. On top of a matching
cherry-wood dresser, her ribbons and trophies sat. Nearly
every one of them was for a beauty pageant she had won.
Age 5. Age 6. Age 7. Age 8. Nautical Cherub Club
Competition. First National and Trust Pageant. Woodbury
County Beauty Contest. The list went on. It had been four
years since she'd entered a contest. After joining Superkid
Academy, she'd put her participation in public beauty competitions on hold. Admittedly, she did miss it a little.

But Missy had learned a lot about *true* beauty. It really
was what was on the inside that counted. She remembered
the Bible story of Samuel looking for a king. He looked at
man after man without success. Then he saw young David.
Everyone had dismissed David. But God hadn't. God re-
minded Samuel that while people look at outside appearances,

He looks at their hearts. And God had especially chosen David...because the boy had a heart after God.

"Charm is deceitful, beauty is vain," Missy whispered to her reflection, remembering Proverbs 31:30. "But a woman who fears the Lord shall be praised." She let go of her hair and it fell around her shoulders. Missy put down the hairbrush and walked over to her nightstand. Sitting on top was the green and red invitation her mother had given her at dinner.

"Miss Nautical Christmas Pageant," it said. "December 24, 5-8 p.m." Then at the bottom: "Final entries due December 23 by 3 p.m. practice. Entry forms may be picked up at area merchants or at the door."

Missy's eyes drifted back to the mirror. She straightened her figure and looked at herself for a long moment. She smiled and then tore the card in half once and again, tossing it into a small wastebasket by her vanity.

With a yawn she tried to hold back, Missy crawled into bed and pulled up the covers. She reached over to the light on her nightstand and tapped it, throwing the room into darkness.

The Superkid closed her eyes and slowly drifted off to sleep...

A sudden whisper. "Missy?"

Missy shot up in bed and slapped on her light. "Who's there?" she demanded.

Missy pushed back the covers and jumped out of bed. She peeked into her bathroom and behind the shower curtain. Moving back into her room, she bent down, peering under her bed. The room was empty. A chill swept down her spine. She walked over and pulled the drapes back from the window. It was pitch black outside. A small, red light signified that the window was locked tight. She pushed the glass with her fingertips just to make sure. It was cold.

The light by her door was red, too. Only her parents had the override for the electronic lock. Missy walked over to it and pushed the open button. The door slid open with a soft hush. She scanned both sides of the hall. All was quiet. She toyed with the idea of knocking on Paul's or Rapper's doors, just a few rooms down. But she decided against it. She didn't want them to think she was a complete basket case—especially after bringing up her troubles twice earlier.

She closed the door, locked it and crawled back into bed. She plopped her head back on her pillow and stared up at the ceiling. Boy, was she worked up. Now she was hearing things.

"Jesus," she prayed in a whisper, "please take this

worry from me. I know You overcame worry when You
died on the cross for me, so I don't have to have it. I give it
over to You. I trust in You. According to 1 Corinthians
15:27, I know all evil principalities and powers are under
Your feet. I rest in that tonight. In Jesus' Name, I thank
You, Father God. Amen."

Missy lay silent for a moment. Then she reached over
and touched the light. The room was dark again. She stared
into the darkness for a while, hearing her own heartbeat.

▲　▲　▲

Missy didn't know which startled her first: the thunder-
ing crash or her mother's scream. Instantly awake, she
leapt out of bed, finding her way easily by the first morning
light. She grabbed her white bathrobe off her vanity chair
and smacked the door open button. Shoving her arms into
her robe, she ran down the hall.

Missy was pretty sure the crash came from downstairs. She rushed down the hallway, the pictures of her family zipping past on both sides.

Shoom! Shoom! Missy heard Paul's and Rapper's doors open, and she heard them fall in behind her. She met the stairs at the same time as her father, coming from a hallway on the other side of the house. He stopped and looked at Missy, clearly wondering if she had caused the crash and screamed. She didn't say a word, but grabbed the banister and shot down the stairs, answering his question: No, it wasn't her. It was her mother.

Single file, Missy, her father, Paul and Rapper bolted down the stairs, three at a time. Missy felt such alarm— hearing her mother scream was a new experience…one Missy didn't like.

Exiting a small hallway, Missy froze in her tracks. Mr. Ashton, Paul and Rapper nearly plowed her over as they stopped. Lois Ashton was motionless, staring forward with a look of fright on her face. At her feet, a silver tray lay atop a shattered china teacup and saucer. Tea was splattered on her slippers, matting and coloring the furry, white cloth. The sandy-colored carpet had already soaked up whatever liquid had hit the floor.

Mr. Ashton pushed in front of Missy and approached his wife. He reached a tender hand behind her back. He began to ask her what was troubling her when he stopped mid-sentence. He looked straight ahead, too…and became speechless.

Missy wanted to ask what was wrong, but couldn't find the words. She walked forward slowly, unsure of what her eyes were about to see. What could be so—

Missy saw it and her heart seemed to skip inside her chest. Her mouth went dry and her eyes teared up. It had to be a joke. Someone was pulling a prank. Had to be. *Had* to be. Behind her, she heard Paul and Rapper gasp.

Every present was gone.

And the beautiful holo-tree had been changed to a lifeless, leafless tree, barren and cold.

Mr. Ashton turned and looked at Paul and Rapper. They both shook their heads. This was no joke. "Someone broke into our house," he said hoarsely.

"I can't—who would—" Lois Ashton couldn't finish a sentence.

"It doesn't make sense," Paul offered. "Someone just

came in and stole your presents? Nothing else is missing, is it?"

Everyone looked around the room. Everything—the expensive picture frames, the furniture, even the marble Nativity scene—was still in place.

"I was just in the kitchen," Mrs. Ashton said, "and nothing—" Suddenly she turned to her husband. "The safe!"

Mr. Ashton blinked and then turned and ran down the hall. He threw open the basement door and sprinted down the steps.

Missy turned to Paul and softly explained, "Mommy and Daddy always put our biggest and most expensive presents in the safe. Downstairs."

Rapper's eyebrows went up. "Man, and I thought you had a lot of presents before."

The sound of Mr. Ashton's steps preceded him. They were all staring down the hall until he reached the top of the stairs. Then he said, "It's all right. Whoever it was didn't know about the safe. Either that or they couldn't get into it. Everything's there."

"How'd they get in without us hearing?" Missy's mother wondered. "We had the alarm system on, didn't we?"

Mr. Ashton looked into the kitchen. "It's *still* on," he

said. "Whoever it was knew what they were doing. I'm calling the police."

Paul bent down and started gathering the broken china.

Missy stared at the tree, barren of green, barren of life. The beautiful white lights were gone. The gold and crystal decorations were gone. The colorful presents were gone. *Who would…?*

A cold chill swept over Missy—like the chill that had swept over her mother the night before.

As her father headed for the ComPhone, Missy said, "It won't matter."

Lois Ashton turned to her daughter, tears in her eyes. "Honey, someone broke into our house. We have to call the police."

Missy shook her head. She bit her upper lip. "No," she said. "It won't matter because they won't find anything."

"Do you know something about this?" her mother asked.

"This was done by a real professional," Missy stated. "It was Mashela."

Paul let out a long breath, looking up. "Missy."

She turned and looked him in the eye. "I know she did this."

"Look, I know you've been through a lot with her—"

"You're still sticking up for her after all she's done?"

Paul stood up, shifting the broken teacup pieces in his hands. "Missy, it's just that not *everything* is Mashela's fault."

"She was in my room last night."

"What?!" Paul, Rapper and Mrs. Ashton said at once.

"I didn't see her, but I heard her. By the time I checked out my whole room, she was gone. But I heard her. I'm telling the truth."

"You didn't hear her come or go?"

"No and—I know it doesn't make sense, but she said my name. She was in my room."

Paul looked at Rapper, who shrugged.

Mrs. Ashton was wiping her eyes. "Are you sure, Missy?"

"I—I think so." She looked at Paul. Then back at the barren holo-tree. "Yes, I'm sure."

"Missy," Paul whispered, touching her arm. She jerked away. She wasn't going crazy. The more she thought about it, the more convinced she was that the voice she'd heard was Mashela's. And Mashela *could* do this. Mashela *would* do this.

Mr. Ashton came around the corner and took his wife in his arms. He rubbed her back as he said, "The police will be here shortly to investigate." He nodded to Missy and said with disgust, "Please turn that holofilm off."

Missy nodded and walked over to the barren tree. If

Missy hadn't known Commander Kellie had already left
Superkid Academy for her own Christmas vacation, she'd
have returned right then to track Mashela down. Track her
down and stop her. She slammed the switch on the oval disc
with her foot.

Pop! The tree disappeared in a flash of light and suddenly in its place stood—*Mashela!* Missy lurched back in
surprise and toppled onto her backside.

"Well, hello there, Christmas beauty!" Mashela
greeted with a wide smile. She was wearing a frumpy, red
Santa Claus suit, complete with a shiny, black belt. Her
curly, black hair dangled out from under a bent hat. As
Missy's head cleared she realized it wasn't Mashela—but
a hologram of her. Mashela had programmed herself into
a holofilm and replaced their Christmas tree program with
her own.

"Pardon me for doing a little Robin-Hooding. Just didn't
seem right that there are *so* many poor people out there
while you *Christians* sit in your warm house and open your
expensive presents. I looked and, to tell you the truth, they
weren't all that great anyway. Your mother totally missed it
on a sweater she bought you. Yellow and orange just aren't
your colors."

Mr. Ashton said, "What *is* this?!"

"Daddy," Missy said, rising. "Meet Mashela Knavery—my thorn in the flesh."

Mashela continued. "I know what you're thinking. No big deal. You weren't attached to those presents—those *things*. Really? Then just think about your reaction when you found out they were missing. You can replace them if you want. Please do. I could use more. Oh—and don't even try to beat me. Remember, I'm well-trained and much sneakier than you since I don't have to worry about my 'Christian' convictions." Her brown eyes grew big. "I don't have any."

"Lord, give me wisdom," Missy whispered Proverbs 2:6.

"Well, I'd better go. I'll keep in touch. Count on it." With that, the recorded hologram of Mashela reached down, then paused. She looked back up at Missy. Then, when she knew she had Missy's attention, she lifted up her right hand and winked. Missy's gift ring from Paul—on Mashela's finger—shone in the light. "Still love me?" And the hologram disappeared. The corner of the room was entirely vacant, save the small, green disc on the floor.

A short silence swept over the room. Finally, Paul said, "OK, so maybe it was Mashela who did this." Missy's mouth dropped.

"Well, I don't like this Mush-ela one bit," Mr. Ashton admitted.

"Muh-shay-la, Daddy," Missy corrected.

Lois Ashton shook her head. "Who is this girl, Missy? I knew she gave you trouble, but…"

"She's *walking* trouble," Missy said, feeling determination rise up inside her. She gritted her teeth. "Stealing, threatening Trouble with a capital 'T.'"

"Is this the kind of thing you deal with at Superkid Academy?" Mrs. Ashton asked.

"Only on the really bad days," Rapper pitched in.

Paul shook his head. "She's gone too far. She's not the person I once knew. What is this all about anyway?"

"All I know," Gregg Ashton said, "is that we need a better security system."

A chuckle escaped Rapper's chest. "You need a dog."

▲　▲　▲

In a lot of places around the country, the police forces and military forces had begun to see internal corruption. Missy knew this because, living at Superkid Academy, she knew what NME was up to. NME stood for Notoriously Malicious Enterprises, which perfectly described the kinds of things NME did: anything malicious. They were the ones

who had found Mashela at a young age and trained her in
their ways. They'd trained her to carry out their operations.
Now, having lost face with them after her brief capture at
Superkid Academy, Mashela was on her own. At least that's
what Missy figured the case to be. She was too prideful to
go back to NME immediately. But they had taught her well.
She knew how to survive on her own, how to live on her
own, and, of course, how to cause trouble. Missy realized
that recently, she had discovered how bad NME really
was—because she saw their beliefs in Mashela.

In Missy's hometown of Nautical, though, the police
corruption wasn't that bad. It helped that her father owned
so much of the city. He had a strong influence in town matters. Somehow, Missy knew, he was a big part of keeping
Nautical a safe place to live.

The police officers who showed up—a man and a
woman—seemed nice enough, but they didn't discover anything Missy didn't already know. There were no finger-
prints, no signs of forced entry, no clues that might lead
them closer to Mashela. The male officer wanted to rope off
the room with police tape and bring in a whole team to
scour it, but Missy's dad refused. He didn't want their
house to look like a story on the evening news. Besides, he
said, they knew who'd done it. Now it was up to them to

catch her. The officers assured the Ashtons they would do
their best. Missy knew, in this case, that their "best" probably wouldn't be enough. Mashela had evaded the authorities for years—why should this year be any different?

Missy told the officers the story about how she was
"connected" with Mashela. She told them how she had only
met the girl a couple months before. Mashela had kidnapped Alex and beaten him up pretty badly. But Alex had
freed himself, capturing Mashela in the process. Mashela
was then relocated to Superkid Academy, where she was
kept in holding until she was to be brought to trial. That's
when Missy met her. She'd had to deliver Mashela food.
And Mashela had begun to taunt her. If that wasn't enough,
it turned out Paul had known Mashela from childhood—
they were both at the same orphanage for a couple years.
Knowing Paul and Missy were close friends, Mashela had
used this to her advantage. She'd offended Missy more than
once and had stolen Missy's ring—the ring Paul had given
her. She'd used it to escape. Now, two months later, she was
still taunting Missy, and Missy didn't exactly know why.
Missy had told Mashela she'd forgiven her. She'd shared
the Truth of God's Word with Mashela—how Jesus died for
her and loved her and rose again for her. She actually
thought she'd gotten through to her. But apparently she

hadn't, because she was still causing trouble. And Missy couldn't figure out why.

"Hey," Paul interrupted her interview. The Nativity scene caught his eye. "Isn't your Nativity scene missing something?" he asked.

Rapper looked at the animals standing around the manger. "Did Mashela get your goat?"

Mr. Ashton, Mrs. Ashton, Paul and Missy all looked at him. He smiled weakly. "Just a...badly timed joke," he said apologetically.

Missy scanned the Nativity scene carefully.

"No, it's not missing anything," Missy told Paul.

Slowly Paul added, "But isn't there supposed to be a baby Jesus in the manger?"

Mrs. Ashton smiled and looked at Missy to provide the answer.

"Not yet," she simply said. "We don't put it out until Christmas Eve. Then, when we awake on Christmas morning, the set is complete."

Paul nodded. He didn't ask anything else about it, so the answer must have satisfied him.

Missy told the officers that was about it. Paul offered a few tidbits about Mashela's childhood, but the officers didn't take notes. Missy thought they looked pretty puzzled. Welcome to Mashela's world of nonsense.

As the officers left, Missy realized how hungry she was. The family and friends had a quiet breakfast together, and then each departed to their room to get ready for the day.

Beautified, Missy returned downstairs an hour later to find Paul and Rapper eating sandwiches at the kitchen table. Her mother was talking to a friend on the Com-Phone, giving her the troublesome details of the morning's encounter. She told her friend to hold on when Missy entered.

"You want me to make you a sandwich, Tootle?" she asked.

Missy shook her head as she pulled back a chair. "I'm still full from breakfast." Her mother went back to her conversation.

Missy turned to Paul and Rapper. "You guys just don't fill up, do you?" Rapper grinned and shook his head.

Missy sat back in her chair. "What an awful way to start the day."

Paul took a drink of milk and said, "It hasn't started out well, but it'll be all right. Your dad told me he can replace the presents, no problem. No one can steal Christmas from you unless you let them. Isn't that what you said?"

Missy felt a pout coming on. "I meant that figuratively," she said.

"What's the difference?"

"The difference is that…well…"

Paul waited.

"The difference is that she stole more than just presents. I know Daddy can replace those. But she also stole our sense of security. Our house has been invaded."

"You know, though, that your security isn't in this house, right? Your security is found in the Lord. Under the shadow of His wings—Psalm 91. Pray Psalm 91 when you feel threatened. Satan can't stand up to that."

Missy knew Paul was right. She knew Psalm 91. She had planted it in her heart as a child. All this mess just had her on edge.

"Look," Paul said after another bite, "I've been thinking."

"Wow," Rapper interjected, his mouth full. Paul ignored him.

"The orphanage I grew up in isn't far from here. Let's go and visit Gran. She helped raise Shea—sorry, Mashela—for a couple years. Maybe she knows something we don't. Maybe she can give us some insight as to why Mashela's doing this."

Missy's mother turned to the three Superkids. "Missy,

if you can find something out, maybe it would help."

Missy jumped up. "All right. Let's go. Let's do it."

Paul smiled and wiped his mouth with a paper napkin. He pushed his chair back.

"You coming, Rap?" he asked.

"Nah, you guys go ahead."

"Good," Mrs. Ashton said. "I need your help with something. And Missy, maybe you can pick up that last present for your Christmas Angel while you're out."

"What about *our* presents?" Missy wondered.

"It's all right. Daddy and I can replace them. Then Daddy'll put them in the safe until Christmas."

Missy let out a long breath. "This is *so* my fault."

Mrs. Ashton turned to the ComPhone screen. "Let me call you back," she said to the caller. Then she walked over to Missy and looked her in the eyes, baby blues to baby blues.

"This is *not* your fault," she said.

"No, it is. I provoked Mashela. If I hadn't gotten offended at her talking to Paul, she wouldn't have caused so much trouble. And maybe Paul could have even ministered to her."

"Tootle, what Mashela did is Mashela's fault. It's not yours. Everything she has done has been her decision. Your daddy and I know that. I don't know why she's not letting it go now, but it's something for which she's going to be accountable before God."

"Doesn't make it much easier," Missy stated. "I just can't bear it that Daddy has to buy all new presents."

Paul jumped in. "We're going to find out what this is all about, Missy. I promise."

Missy nodded. "OK. I'm ready."

Paul smiled. "Then let's go fire up the GRXs."

▲   ▲   ▲

When the garage door opened, she dodged around the side of the house. This was so predictable. Missy has trouble and, instead of retreating, she starts meddling in other people's business. Fine. Let her waste her time. It wasn't like she was going to discover anything anyway. And if she did, well, then she'd have to be taught another life lesson.

Mashela rolled her eyes. All she had wanted to do was stir things up and then steal away Missy's Christmas. Now it was turning into more, because Missy was retaliating. *Fine. We'll fight fire with fire,* she thought.

"I feel like someone's following us," Missy said into her ComWatch. Paul sped down the road—his GRX air scooter in front of hers. Missy always preferred GRXs to other scooters since they were as quiet as the wind and fairly comfortable. Of course, the helmets always messed up her hair...

Paul's face popped up on her ComWatch. "I haven't seen anyone for miles," he said through its small screen.

"Just a feeling."

This time of year, Missy was extra thankful her dad owned Ashton Clothiers. She always had more than enough warm clothes for cold days like this. Both she and Paul wore Ashton Signature GRX gear over their sweatshirts and jeans. The gear was comprised of a bright, neon-blue coat and pants—both thick and warm.

Missy's hometown of Nautical was fading in her rear-view mirror. A little more than an hour had passed. In the distance, they saw Sawyer approaching. On the outskirts of town stood a small, two-story, gray house: Sawyer Orphanage. It was hard for Missy to imagine growing up here. Paul had done it. Many kids had. But the concept seemed foreign to Missy. She'd grown up in a ritzy, suburban dwelling, complete with anything she'd ever needed. This seemed so drastically different. Well, it *was* so drastically different.

The two Superkids pulled into a small driveway outside the house. Missy skillfully dodged a few ice slicks that hadn't managed to melt yet. It felt good to get off the bike and stretch her legs. She unfastened her helmet and felt the chilly wind bite her cheeks. Too bad it was overcast. A little sun would have been nice.

Missy did feel a little warmth when she saw the bright green wreath on the front door, just a little bit off-center. Suddenly the door flew open and there was old Gran, with a big, toothy smile. She was a short, rosy-cheeked woman with beautiful, wrinkly, dark skin and a wide frame.

"Paul Temp, is that you?!" she exclaimed. "C'mon inside 'fore you get cold!"

"It's Paul West now," Paul said, with a chuckle. Missy walked up the steps as Paul pushed from behind. "You remember Missy, don't you, Gran?"

"Of course I do. How can I forget a pretty face like that?" She winked at Missy. She shut the door, cutting off the cold. "You want some cherry lemonade?"

"I was hoping you'd ask," Paul said. Missy nodded. When she had met Gran a few months before, she'd had her first taste of the woman's famous, homemade cherry lemonade. It was sweet and sour and wonderful.

Gran departed to the kitchen, grabbing the hand of a 3-year-old on her way. Paul took off his GRX gear and Missy followed suit. It felt nice to escape the layers of fabric.

Out of the small, shabby entryway and into the halls, strings of silver garland accented the walls. There was something so inviting about it. It was Christmas.

Missy followed Paul to the kitchen, passing a small playroom with three children inside. Each one had their toy of choice in front of them or in their laps, contentedly creating new worlds.

The kitchen was small, too, and just as Missy had last seen it. A little dusty, but comfortable. She slid into a chair next to Paul, both of them sitting opposite Gran. As they sipped on their lemonade, Gran doted on Paul, telling Missy some of the same stories she'd told her last time she was there. Saying that she had been a caretaker for more than 20 years, taken care of more than 60 children and that Paul was her favorite one. So were all the others, Paul assured Missy.

Then Paul brought Gran up to date on his life. He told

her how he'd found out the truth about his parents: how
they had known the Ashtons and been covenant friends with
Missy's parents. And how Mr. and Mrs. Ashton had made
Paul feel like their own. Missy could listen to the story
time and again. It made her feel so rewarded to have been a
part of it. She could tell he was just as excited about his
new family today as ever. Under the table, Missy rubbed her
right ring finger, feeling the spot where her ring should be.
It was a "Thank You" gift Paul had given her…one that
meant a lot. Maybe one day when Mashela was behind bars,
she would get it back. Missy shook her head. *No.* She had
to keep from being offended at Mashela. She'd learned that
lesson once and didn't want to mess up again. She silently
prayed that Mashela would realize how much she was hurting Missy and stop what she was doing. It was actually
hard for Missy to pray that prayer—it seemed such an
impossibility. But as Mark 10:27 says, all things are pos-
sible with God.

As if reading Missy's mind, Gran said, "Well, Paul, if I
know you, you haven't come here for just a friendly visit."
She turned to Missy. "He's always got a goal. Something he
has to find out."

Paul chuckled. "Well, it's true. I do have an ulterior
motive." Then Paul told Gran about Mashela. He told her

about Mashela's kidnapping Alex, her capture and escape, her kidnapping Rapper and threatening Missy. As he spoke, Gran listened intently, her gray eyes revealing her sadness.

When Paul finished, he asked Gran if there was anything she could tell them that would help them find Mashela, or at least understand her. Gran sat in silence. Then, finally, "I wish I could say something. But, Paul, I can't. I'm not supposed to reveal anything personal about my orphans. That's part of running an orphanage."

"Not even if it could help her?" Paul asked.

Gran shook her head.

"You know she's lost, Gran. There has to be something we can do. We need to get her off the streets, out of NME's hands and into counseling. That's her only hope. She's on a path leading to destruction."

"Dear Shea…"

Paul looked into Gran's watery, gray eyes.

"I'm sorry."

Paul let out a long, low breath in frustration.

"I understand," Missy said softly. "We can't ask you to break the rules. But thank you anyway. God will show us the answer. I'm sure of it."

Paul nodded. He leaned across the table and cupped his hands over Gran's. "I understand, too."

"And the lemonade—great stuff," Missy chimed in. The three smiled.

"Well, I guess we'd better get going," Paul said, looking at his ComWatch. Missy looked at hers. More than an hour had passed. "We have to buy a present and get back before dinner." Paul stood up and headed toward the entryway. Missy followed. Gran, still silent, was close behind.

As the Superkids began putting on their GRX gear, Gran suddenly spoke up.

"You know," she said, "I'm getting old."

Missy looked at Paul. Paul looked at Missy.

She continued, "Sometimes old people mumble to themselves about people they know. Things they know."

Gran turned as she said, "I'm going to go make dinner now."

Paul and Missy watched her scoot down the hall.

"What do we do?" Missy whispered.

Paul only hesitated for a moment. "We follow her," he said, pulling his leg gear back off. He started down the hall and Missy was right behind him.

Gran headed around the corner, into the living room/playroom, checking in on the three children playing with their toys on her way through. She moved across the room, gathering scattered toys from the floor.

"Mashela Knavery," she said to no one in particular. "Now there's a name I don't know. I only knew a young lady by the name of Shea Brown. She was a hurting girl, always searching for love. A troublemaker, oh *Lord,* a troublemaker. But still a young girl. Searching for love."

She opened a wooden toy chest at the back of the room. Paul and Missy stayed silent at the room's entrance.

"This little orphanage was Shea's third home. NME took her from her family when she was just a toddler. I'm not sure why. I don't suppose I'll ever know. But they put her into the care of a foster family." Gran stopped moving as she said, *"Care.* I wouldn't call it that. Those people *didn't* love her. Didn't respect her. Didn't raise her properly. That's why the authorities delivered her to my orphanage."

Gran slipped passed them and walked into the kitchen. They followed. She grabbed their lemonade glasses off the table. Turning to the sink, she washed them by hand.

"Me, I did my best. Kept Shea safe for two years. Paul was here then." Gran chuckled. "Now there was a trouble-some duo. Shea and Paul. Paul and Shea. Couldn't keep them apart."

Missy looked at Paul, who stared straight ahead. She couldn't begin to understand what Mashela would be like as a friend. But Paul did. To this day, though he'd seen her cause so much trouble, he couldn't help but defend her once in a while. Paul was a true friend—he believed the best for her all the time. *Didn't she realize she was hurting him by hurting his friends?*

Gran was still talking. "Then one day, two NME agents show up. I had no choice. They had all the legal papers. And they took Shea away. I knew they were recruiting her. Going to train her in their evil ways. NME was less known then, but there were rumors. I didn't doubt the rumors. No good mother would.

"But I always wondered what I could have done different. Sixty children I've raised and not a one of them is a bad kid. Just good kids with bad ideas put in their heads. I'll tell you, if I could do it differently, I could only love more. Love them more…love her more. Love is the only key, I think, to reaching a cold heart. And her heart is cold, indeed."

Gran finished the dishes without another word. Paul tapped Missy on the shoulder and they both went back out into the entryway.

"She's had a hard life, hasn't she?" Missy said.

"I never realized she was kidnapped from her parents," Paul noted. "The only parents she ever told me about were her foster parents. She has more secrets than I knew."

"I hope Gran's right," Missy stated. "Love may be the only way to reach her. If not love, I'm out of ideas. Love her despite what she does...or why she does it."

They put their GRX gear on. "Have you ever noticed," Missy said, "that there seem to be more questions about Mashela than answers?"

"Maybe that's because we're looking for answers where there are none," Paul said.

"Hmm."

Paul reached for the door open button.

"Shouldn't we say goodbye?" Missy wondered.

Paul shook his head. "As far as Gran is concerned, we left 10 minutes ago."

▲ ▲ ▲

Up on a hill, Mashela sat sulking, staring blankly at the little orphanage she'd spent a couple years in. As far as she was concerned, it had been her only home and because of that, she didn't blame Gran for telling them. But she did blame Missy for asking. That Superkid. Thinks love is the answer to everything. Mashela expected that from a senile old woman, but a teenager?

She watched them exit the front door and get on their scooters.

We'll see, she thought. *Soon.*

▲   ▲   ▲

As they boarded their air scooters, Missy said, "You know what's sad? Mashela's like she is because of how she's been forced to live. Good kid with bad ideas put in her head."

Paul turned to Missy. He looked at the ground and then back at her. "I don't know. Personally, my sympathy's running out. She's got a smart head on her shoulders. No one's forcing her to live this way anymore."

"What about me?"

"What about you?"

"Am I the way I am just because my parents put good things in my head?"

Paul didn't miss a beat. "Missy, why did you agree to come out here with me today?"

Missy paused. "To...I don't know...find out more about Mashela. See if there's some way we can help her."

"After all she's done, you want to help her?!"

"Well, I want to stop her, too. But...yes. I want to help her."

"No one's forcing you to feel that way, Missy. That's just you. That's who you've become in the Lord. We are both new creations according to 2 Corinthians 5:17. New from the inside out. What's in our past no longer matters. We are the way we are because we choose to live this way, not because we grew up the right way. We're choosing life."

Missy felt her throat tightening. "I'm so thankful, Paul," she said. "I'm so thankful I've made the right choices. My decisions are what separate me from Mashela. And that's it. I've chosen to follow the Lord. To live right. So many teenagers don't. But through God's grace I did." Then, "So what's going to happen to Mashela?"

Paul was still. "I don't know. But I know it's not too late. She can change today if she wants to. God will accept her. God can use her. Isaiah 49:1 says He named her while she was in her mother's womb. He has a plan for her."

Missy quickly wiped her fingers underneath her eyes. The chilly air dried them before she could put her gloves on. "Let's go," she said. "It's so cold out."

Paul nodded. "We still need to get another present for your Christmas Angel?"

Missy's eyes lit up as she pushed heavier thoughts aside. "Yeah, that's right. I wonder if there's any place around here we can get something."

"Back in Nautical there's that collectibles shop with all those stuffed bears. Remember?"

"How could I forget? We blew up the building across the street," Missy said with a smile. "You think the owner will be happy to see us?"

Paul pulled down his visor. "There's one way to find out. Besides, what's the worst that can happen?"

Indeed, Mashela thought.

"Aaaagh!"

Mr. Fifopolis, the owner of Fiffer's Crafts and Collectibles, nearly fell back into the boxes stacked behind him.

"You all right?" Missy asked.

"You! You-you-you-you're the ones—"

Paul interrupted, "Who helped you clear away the building across the street. Yeah, that's us."

Mr. Fifopolis gulped loudly.

"You know that wasn't actually us—it was that thief who followed us."

Mr. Fifopolis nodded slowly. He craned his neck toward the door. "Anyone follow you this time?"

Missy looked at Paul for the answer. He changed the subject.

"It looks like you're packing up shop."

It was true. Mr. Fifopolis had boxes stacked all around the store, presumably packed with inventory. The Superkids had seen the building across the street on the way in. It looked nearly finished, ready for

Fiffer's to change storefronts.

"Almost ready to move," he said. "Just a couple more daisy-do's here."

A customer, a small man, looking somewhat like the Santa bear in his hand, approached the counter. Mr. Fifopolis totaled his purchase. As the man walked out the door, Missy approached the counter. "Do you have a sign-up sheet for the Miss Nautical Christmas Pageant?"

Paul, who had started down an aisle, stopped and turned. Missy felt a rush of embarrassment hit her. Now she'd have to explain.

"You're kidding," Paul said.

"I wish," she replied flippantly. Maybe she *didn't* have to explain. Paul knew her pretty well. And he knew it was upsetting to her that her dad had to replace all the presents. Paul also knew Missy would want to find her own way to replace those presents. The Miss Nautical Christmas Pageant seemed the perfect vehicle.

Mr. Fifopolis scrounged under the counter and came up with a legal-sized pad of paper. He tore off a sheet and handed it to Missy. She accepted it and glanced over the black and white entry form. Standard stuff: Name, birth date, ambitions. She quickly folded it up and shoved it through her gear and into her jeans pocket.

When she turned, she walked along the front of the
store, looking for Paul. No one else appeared to be inside,
except a big Frosty the Snowman cardboard display in front
of aisle five. She finally found Paul in the third aisle, comparing teddy bears. There were at least 50 different ones.
They were all somewhat similar, but different colors. And
each one was a different profession: doctor, lawyer, fisher-
man and more.

"These are kinda cute," he offered. Missy agreed.
Carpenter, teacher, golfer—all cute, but none seemed quite
right for a Christmas Angel.

▲   ▲   ▲

Mashela smirked. The pageant was an interesting
development. She'd think about that. Quietly, she slid into
the small collectibles store and scooted to the first aisle.
The old man at the counter didn't even notice her. She
made her way to the back. The main power line had to be
somewhere near.

▲   ▲   ▲

Suddenly, a chill crawled down Missy's spine. She
looked up and around. "Lord, are You trying to show me
something?" she whispered.

"Huh?" Paul asked.

"What? Oh. Nothing," Missy said, looking around one last time.

ZzzzZzzzZzzzZzzzZzzz…

Missy turned around to spy a small, silver ball ornament rolling toward her. It bobbed against her foot and stopped. Paul didn't seem to notice. Missy cautiously reached down and picked it up. It was perfectly round and shiny, with a knob on the top where the hook attached. She could see her reflection in it. In fact, she could see Paul's reflection behind her. And Mashela's reflection behind him.

Missy's mouth went dry. "P…Paul," she whispered, holding perfectly still.

"Awesome!" Paul shouted. Missy spun around—and nearly fell. Paul caught her arm. "You all right?"

Missy looked behind him. No one was there.

"Missy, you're white as a sheet."

"She's following us," Missy stated.

"Who? Mashela?"

"Uh-huh."

"Where?"

"I just saw her in here. I…think I did."

"OK. I believe you. After last night, let's not take any chances."

"Why's she doing this, Paul?"

"Let's hope you don't have a chance to ask her."

Paul held up a bear. It had curly, brown fur and wore a baseball uniform. "Let's get this bear for your Christmas Angel and get out of here. This isn't the time or place for a confrontation."

"Deal."

Missy grabbed the bear and swiftly exited the aisle, moving toward the cash register. Paul stayed close behind, scanning the aisles as he walked. Missy smiled at Mr. Fifopolis and placed the bear on the counter.

"Ooo. Excellent choice," he said, patting the bear on its head. "One of my favorites." He carefully wrapped it in thin, red and green striped paper and placed it in a plain, brown bag. He accepted Missy's payment and handed her the sack. "See?" he said. "That wasn't so hard. You came in and bought something without a hitch." He winked at Missy.

Suddenly the lights went off.

"Oh, boy," Fifopolis said with dismay.

With the overcast sky outside, it was darker than ex--pected—even with the big windows at the front of the shop. Paul shouted out, "Mashela?!"

"I can explain," Missy offered to Fifopolis. "You

see, it started back—"

"I need to call the police, don't I?"

"It wouldn't be a bad idea."

Fifopolis shuffled into a small room behind the counter. Missy turned to Paul. "Let's get out of here. She has the advantage over us."

Paul grabbed Missy's hand and headed to the door. It didn't slide open. Missy looked at her friend. "Déjà vu, huh?"

"She turned the power off."

"There has to be a manual override," Missy said, pushing a small button on the wall. Nothing happened.

"Where's your bear?"

Missy looked down. She didn't have it. She looked back at the sales counter. The brown bag still sat on top. Paul saw it, too.

"I'll go get the bear," he said, already moving. "You find a way to open this door."

Missy pushed the button three more times and gave up. She scoured the wall for another switch.

Paul reached the counter and grabbed the bag. Suddenly a shadow slid across the floor near aisle 13. Missy saw him pause. Then he shook his head and started toward Missy.

Pow!

Pow! Pow! Pow!

Pow! Pow!

Paul twirled around, dropping the bag. He turned sideways in defense and bent over as small ornaments came at him like bullets. He dodged them as best he could, but took several in his back. Missy, eyes wide, thanked God he was wearing the thick GRX gear.

Pow! Pow!

Pow! Pow! Pow!

As Paul dodged more blows, Missy ran to aisle five and snatched Frosty the Cardboard Snowman from his post. She threw him down flat and pushed as hard as she could. The big, cardboard cartoon character slid across the floor like a snow sled, and landed at Paul's feet. He reached down and picked him up, using the snowman as a makeshift shield.

Pow! Pow! Pow!

Sorry, Frosty.

Missy took off down the aisle and came out at the back of the store. She ran past three, four, five aisles. There! She anchored her feet when she saw Mashela standing in the middle of aisle 10, holding a toy gun loaded with ornament bullets.

Thump! Missy's right foot toppled over her left as she miscalculated her stance. Suddenly, she was falling sideways, into a 7-foot display of "Blinking Rudolph Noses"— fun for the whole family.

Wham! The metal display shot every which way—the flashing, red noses scattering like marbles. Missy jumped to her feet and froze. Mashela was gone.

She looked behind her. Nothing but blinking noses.

At the other end of the aisle, she could see Paul peeking out from behind Frosty the Dented Snowman.

Why is she doing this? Missy wondered.

"She's not getting out," Paul said, energized from the sudden rush of adrenaline. He disappeared, heading toward the door.

Missy took a deep breath and let it out. She heard the Holy Spirit remind her of Romans 12:18: *As far as it depends on you, live at peace with everyone.* She had to keep perspective. She remembered the little girl who'd been kidnapped. The little girl who'd been tossed between foster homes and the orphanage. She was a person...a person who needed compassion. A person who needed love. A person who needed Jesus.

"Mashela," she said aloud. "We can talk about this. I forgive you. I do. I don't want to fight."

Missy combed the next two aisles, looking this way and that for any trace of Mashela's presence. She also looked above her—pouncing down was one of the girl's favorite tactics, Missy remembered.

Crunch. Missy looked beneath her foot. The shards of a small, broken ornament lay underneath. Great. They were going to owe Mr. Fifopolis some cleaning-up time after this one.

Crunch. Missy almost lifted her foot again, but then stopped. She hadn't taken a step. She whirled around. On the ground was a small spot of crunched glass.

"Mashela?" Missy called, her voice cracking.

Creeeeee…

The Superkid looked around her. What was that?

Missy barely had time to react. It was the right side of aisle 12. Coming down on her. As the tall, shelving divider came down, Missy sprinted to the end of the aisle, diving out just as it came crashing down to the floor with a *Ka-BAM!*

"Missy!" Paul's face shouted from her ComWatch.

"I'm all right!"

She hopped up again, feeling extremely hot in her GRX gear. She shot down aisle 13. She wasn't even a quarter of the way through when she saw the right wall tumbling in.

She whirled around and escaped again, nearly hitting the back wall. *Ka-BAM!*

She looked at Paul in her ComWatch. "But my compassion is dwindling!"

Missy ran back three aisles to aisle 10. She started down the aisle, seeing the left wall, this time, coming in on her. She ran her hardest to the center of the aisle and grabbed the toppled Rudolph nose display. She hit the deck as she pushed it back as far as she could. *Ka-BAM!* The wall came down, right over Missy. It crunched onto the metal display, but didn't flatten it—or Missy, lying on her stomach beside it.

Paul's face appeared on her ComWatch.

"I'm still all right," she said to him. She crawled on her stomach to the back of the aisle. She planned to exit and run for the door—over aisle 10. But suddenly something blocked her way. No, some*one* blocked her way.

Mashela.

She was crouched down, smiling at Missy, who was still on her stomach, under aisle 10.

"Why are you following us?" Missy had to ask.

"It's not like it's hard."

"Why?"

"Because you stick out like sore thumbs in that

ridiculous gear you're wearing."

"No—I mean *why* are you following us?"

"To make your life miserable."

"Which brings me again to *why?*"

"Because I don't lose."

"You don't lose," Missy said flatly.

"I know. And I'm going to completely ruin your Christmas. I know how much you love it. I know you. Last time we saw each other, you said you loved me because God loves me. Well. I think you don't love me—or at least you won't by the time I'm finished. Your love will fail."

"God's love never fails. First Corinthians 13."

"Blah-blah-blah. We'll see. You'll be easy to break. You're as vain as they come. I know you, Missy. We're the same, remember?"

The shock on Missy's face was evident. "Scuse me?"

"You heard me. We're the same. Look at us. We're both teenagers, highly trained. We're both beautiful."

"Well, *one* of us is anyway," Missy interjected.

"Thank you."

Missy looked up at Mashela. "I was talking about me." She smiled curtly. Mashela smiled back. With her right hand, Missy silently felt around under the shelf. She found a bar to grab.

"But," the ex-NME agent taunted, "you're not beautiful enough to win the Miss Nautical Christmas Pageant."

Missy's mouth fell open. "How'd you know about the pageant? Only my parents and Paul and Rapper know about that."

Mashela smiled. "You'd be surprised what I know, *Tootle*."

Whoosh! Missy threw her weight to the right and threw her lower body out from under the aisle. She spun around on the floor and her legs caught Mashela's, sending her toppling to the ground. Missy jumped to her feet. Mashela jumped to hers, surprise all over her face.

"Didn't expect that, did ya?" Missy asked. "Not all beauty—brains, too."

Paul came running down the back aisle. He stopped when he saw both girls facing off.

"Where've you been?" Missy asked.

"I thought you said you were all right!"

"Well, I was *then!*"

Mashela bolted past Missy, jumping onto the toppled aisle wall. Missy leapt forward, but missed. Paul darted through aisle nine. Mashela shot into eight. Paul and Missy hit eight at the same time and ran after her. They followed her to five, then four, then split up. Before they knew it, they were running down aisles, looking for Mashela again. Suddenly, the electricity came back on and they heard the main store door open and close. The Superkids ran to the front of the store and looked at the door. Frosty was laying on the ground with boot prints right across his corncob pipe, button nose and two eyes made out of coal.

Missy caught her breath as she said, "I thought I had her."

"You almost did."

Missy pulled off her GRX gear. "I'm so HOT!"

Paul took his gear off, too, as he looked around the store, catching his breath. "We're going to be here awhile, aren't we?"

Missy nodded.

Mr. Fifopolis peeked out of his back room. "Is it safe to come out? I called the police, but they're sure taking their time."

Paul motioned that it was OK.

The store owner's mouth dropped as he looked at his store. "Well…I…It's a good thing I'm moving."

"We're going to stay until the last scrap is cleaned up," Missy promised.

"You kids really are something." Mr. Fifopolis shook his head. "Please tell me you at least got the thief this time…"

Missy looked at Paul. Paul looked at Missy.

Mr. Fifopolis shuffled around the counter and said, "Will you two promise me one thing?"

"Anything," Missy said. "And I mean *anything.*"

"If you need something in the future, would you just *call?* I'll put it in the mail."

"What's that smell?" Missy asked, wrinkling her nose as she and Paul entered her house. Paul sniffed the air as he removed his GRX gear. "I don't smell anything."

Missy took off her gear. Her face grimaced. "It's *disgusting.*"

Paul shrugged.

"There you are!" Mrs. Ashton exclaimed from the top of the basement stairs. "We've been waiting for you! You've been gone so long!"

"Sorry we didn't call. We sort of got into a mishap and—"

"C'mon! C'mon!" Mrs. Ashton shouted, motioning. She disappeared into the basement.

Paul chuckled. "Something's always new in the Ashton household."

They walked down the hall to the basement door and Missy entered first, placing a foot on the first stair. Then it came. Like a pouncing lion, it bounded toward her— big, yellow eyes shining. Missy screamed like a monkey.

Boom! It jumped onto her, throwing its paws up on

her shoulders. A huge, pink tongue shot out and slapped her across the face.

"OH! GROOOSSSSS!!!!!!!!!!!" Missy screamed, tumbling backward, pushing the huge dog away. With her eyes shut tight, she shook her hands in front of her. "EW! EW! EW! EW! EW! EW! EW! GROSS! GROSS! GROSS! YUCK! YUCK! YUCK!"

Paul bent down and threw his arms around the big canine. "Awesome! Hey boy!"

"He *is* awesome, isn't he?!" Rapper agreed, now in the hall. Mr. and Mrs. Ashton were back up the stairs, too, smiling big.

Missy was still shaking her hands. "Ew! How did that *beast* get into my house?!"

Mrs. Ashton bent down and petted the dog. "Now, Tootle, don't treat Killer like that. He's yours."

"MINE?! You got me a dog named *'Killer'?!?!"*

"He came with that name," Mrs. Ashton continued. "He does all kinds of tricks! And he's potty trained so you don't have to teach him!"

"You would have made me potty train a dog named *Killer?!"*

Mr. Ashton was petting the dog now, too. "He's here for your protection, dear."

Missy shot her eyes at Rapper. "This was your idea, wasn't it?"

Rapper said, "Anyone for ice cream?" and exited the room.

Paul looked up. "Really, Missy, a dog's not such a bad idea right now."

"And he likes you," Mrs. Ashton said, scratching his ears. She started talking to him like he was a newborn baby: "You like Missy, don't you, Killer? Don't you? Yes, you do!"

The big, black and brown dog was eating up all the attention. His tail slapped against Missy's leg, threatening to bruise it if she stood there long enough.

"A *dog?*" Missy asked no one in particular.

"This breed is supposed to be a great watchdog," Mrs. Ashton said. "The young man at the store said he was very smart, too."

"What breed is he?" Paul asked.

Mr. Ashton answered. "Sort of a Doberman/German shepherd/poodle mix."

Missy looked at her father disbelieving. "Poodle? What kind of watchdog is a poodle?"

"The watchdog is the Doberman/German shepherd part."

"This tops my day," Missy cracked. "My safety is in the

paws of a DobShepPoo named Killer."

"Aw," Mrs. Ashton said, turning the dog's face to meet Missy's. "How can you turn away something so sweet?" The dog's big brown and yellow eyes seemed to water as his tongue hung out.

"OK, if that's what you all want. But I am *so* changing his name."

▲ ▲ ▲

From the kitchen, Missy's mother called for Killer. The DobShepPoo hopped up and trotted into the room, his nails clicking against the tile. She pointed him to his food bowl, but he was heading for it anyway. Missy entered the room with her father and Paul. Rapper was sitting at the table drinking a soda.

"So what happened today, Tootle?" Mrs. Ashton asked.

Missy looked at Paul. Paul looked at Missy.

Mr. Ashton caught the look. "You ran into that Mushela girl, didn't you?"

"Muh-*shay*-la, Daddy," Missy corrected. "Yeah, we did. She followed us into a collectibles shop and nearly tore the place apart. We stayed to help clean up."

Mrs. Ashton walked over and hugged her daughter. She pulled back and looked her in the eyes. "She didn't hurt you, did she?"

"No," Missy said flatly. "We nearly duked it out, but I'm OK. The store took the brunt of it."

Rapper asked, "Where was I during all this?"

"Buying a dog that slobbers."

"Shhh! You'll hurt his feelings."

Missy gave her parents a play-by-play of their day, from the trip to Sawyer Orphanage to the confrontation at Fiffer's.

"So," Missy finalized, "I have a little more compassion for her, knowing all she's been through. But I'm asking God to give me more compassion. What little I have is fading fast under this persecution."

"Did you ever find out why she's doing this?" Mrs. Ashton asked, handing Missy a glass of water.

"I got a clue," Missy admitted.

"You did?" Paul asked.

Missy nodded. "She says she wants to win. She wants to prove my love for her will run out. Last time I confronted her, I told her I wouldn't stop loving her. She's testing me on that. Basically, she's testing Jesus in me."

"Well, you know what Jesus would do?" Mr. Ashton asked.

"He wouldn't stop loving her, that's for sure. Which is

why I need His help in this. I know Luke 6:27-28 says to do good to those who hate us and pray for those who mistreat us. It's just frustrating. Other than testing me, she has no reason for all this trouble."

"Many times, that's the way persecution is," Mr. Ashton pointed out. "No apparent rhyme or reason behind it."

"Satan is the rhyme and reason behind it," Paul said. "He's influencing Mashela. And she's letting him."

"Well, I know how to stop it," Missy responded.

"And that is?"

"I'm going to bless her. Pray for her. And like Gran said, love her. That's what I believe Jesus is telling me to do."

Everyone nodded.

"Well, I've been busy today," Mr. Ashton said, leaning back on the kitchen counter. "Bad news. The second the police chief heard we were looking for Miss Mush-ela, he took his officers off of the case. I don't know why, but it's my guess NME has their claws in him. I knew it was bound to happen sooner or later. Anyway, he gave me some story about how it's our word against hers. If we want to turn her in, they want proof. Otherwise, the longest they can hold her is 24 hours. Et cetera, et cetera. They're giving us the runaround. I won't have it. But it'll take awhile until I can really do something about it. It's the Christmas season and the courts are going out of session."

"So even if we catch her, it won't do any good?"

"Not yet."

"Hmmm. Well, maybe she doesn't need to be caught," Missy said. "I mean, we had her before. She escaped. She'll just escape again anyway."

"What are you suggesting?" Paul wondered.

"I'm suggesting what she needs is a change of heart."

"And how do you do that?"

"I don't. God does. We're going to have to rely on Him, no matter how hard that may seem—especially with her breaking into our house and following us."

Rapper raised his hand. "Um, I for one, really have enjoyed my stay here, but I have to say I'll be glad to get home."

Missy placed her hand on top of Rapper's. "And I, for one, am glad you've been here long enough to get me a slobbering mutt."

Rapper smiled. "My pleasure."

Missy pulled her hand away. "I should make you take him with you when you go."

Rapper looked down at Killer. "I dunno. He looks pretty content here." The dog lifted his head and barked at Missy. She jumped at the loud sound. Everyone laughed.

"Hey!" Paul said. "You going to tell everyone your big news?!"

Missy closed her eyes. She hadn't planned to share it quite yet...

"What?" Mrs. Ashton asked.

"I'm, uh..." Missy's voice faded as she said, "I'm going to enter the Miss Nautical Christmas Pageant."

"Ohhhhhh! My little girl!" Mrs. Ashton squealed, throwing her arms around Missy. Missy smiled. She knew it'd make her mom happy.

Mr. Ashton interrupted. "Missy, you don't have to do this. You know it's not your fault, don't you?"

Missy didn't say anything.

"We don't need the prize money, sweetheart. In fact, I've already replaced all the presents. I put them in the safe with the others."

Paul's eyebrows shot up. "You've already replaced *all* the presents?"

"Daddy has connections," Missy stated. Then, "I know. I just...I want to do this. I'm going to sign up tomorrow at the door, just before the practice. I got an entry form."

Mrs. Ashton was still all smiles. "This will be so much fun! We can watch you win on Christmas Eve and then go to the Christmas Angel dinner afterward. So much fun!

And you'll be on the front page of the Nautical Times!"

"Mommy, that's not why I'm doing this."

"Oh, I know. But it's a nice plus!"

"Aw, man!" Rapper said. "I'm gonna totally miss it. My dad's coming tomorrow. I won't even be able to stick around for the practice. I'm sorry."

"You're being sarcastic, aren't you?" Missy prodded.

Rapper smiled. "No, really, I will miss seeing you win."

Missy smiled back at Rapper. "Well, I'll miss having you there, buddy."

▲ ▲ ▲

The rest of the evening consisted of playing games, eating dessert and vegging out. It was just what Missy needed. At first, she'd found it hard to participate—everyone had—but soon she was as loud as the rest, laughing and kidding and competing for first place. A few hours later, when Missy's parents went to bed, Paul and Rapper decided to stay up and watch a Zoey and Zuzu holiday marathon. Missy opted out, stating that she needed her beauty sleep.

Only at one point did the evening get a bit quiet. It was just after the first round of Parcheesi. Missy was about to send her red token home when suddenly Killer, who had taken up permanent residence in front of the couch, popped his ears up. His head soon followed and he stared out the window into the dark, snowy yard beyond. They didn't think much of it until a low, gurgling growl emerged from his throat and put everyone on edge. Mr. Ashton drew the curtains closed and double-checked the alarm system. It took awhile to get back into Parcheesi after that, but soon they had all but forgotten Killer's alert.

Missy had just finished brushing her hair and she lay down on her bed. She kept the lights on and began to pray. Some people pray on their knees, others while sitting. Missy preferred to just lie back in bed and stare up at the ceiling. She figured God didn't mind how you prayed, as long as you *did* pray.

"Lord God," she prayed, "I choose today to obey Your Word. I'm going to bless Mashela like Romans 12:14 says. I know You crown me with Your love and compassion—Psalm 103:4. I pray they fill me up. God, I really need Your help here—just being honest. It's getting more difficult, the more she does. But I want to love her, I really do. So in the Name of Jesus, I say, 'Satan, get away from her right now!'

"I also pray Philippians 4:7—that she has peace she doesn't understand. Lord, let her experience Your unconditional love. It changed me. I know it can change someone like her, too. Finally, Lord, I thank You for protection.

She's out there, and there's not much we can do about it. So I pray for angels to take charge over us, like Psalm 91:11 says. I pray they watch over us and protect us. God, I know my dad is right. I know I'll face persecution. I just read in 2 Timothy 3:12 that everyone who wants to live a godly life in Jesus will be persecuted. So please help me to do it with the mercy and grace You've shown me. In Jesus' Name. Amen."

Missy let out a long breath and turned off the light. Feeling more at peace and relaxed, she slowly drifted off to sleep...

A sudden whisper. "Missy?"

Missy sat up straight in bed and slapped on the light. "Who's there?"

Missy threw her covers aside and jumped out of bed. She slipped over to her bathroom and checked behind the shower curtain. Then she came back in and looked under her bed. The room was empty.

"You have my attention, Mashela," she said. She stood in the middle of her room waiting for something...anything.

Nothing.

Her eyes moved to the small red light by her window. It was on. The window was locked. Then she moved to her door. The red light was on there, too. Missy pushed the

open button. The door slid open. Her heart skipped a beat
when Killer jumped up. She actually felt relieved when she
realized he had been lying outside her door.

Missy peered down the hall and didn't see anyone.
Killer looked up at her with his big, yellow and brown eyes.
His tail swished in the air. Missy gave in and stood aside.
"C'mon, boy," she coaxed. Killer obediently walked into
her room. She closed the door behind him and got back into
bed. He just stood there, looking at her. She tightened her
lips and looked back at him. Then she patted the foot of her
bed. That was all it took. The big beast jumped onto the end
of her bed and lay across it, his legs dangling off each side.

"Killer," she whispered. He looked up at her. She pointed
her finger at him. "Do not tell anyone I let you up here,
you got that?"

Killer whimpered.

"Good. And you'd better not shed."

Missy lay back and prayed again, thanking God for
His protection and help in time of need. Then she turned
off the light and lay silently for a while, just listening to
Killer breathe.

"You sure you're not doing this because you feel responsible?"

"Paul, no, I—well, OK, maybe a little," Missy said. "I want to do this for my parents. I want to do it for my mom because she wants me to do it so bad. And I want to do it for my dad because…well, the cash prize would be a nice Christmas present for him. To help replace all those presents Mashela stole."

Paul stopped walking and turned to Missy, who also stopped. "You *know* you don't have to do this for their approval. They love you regardless."

"I know," Missy said with a smile. It really wasn't about pleasing them. It was about giving to them—presents they'd always remember. Missy knew her mother would never forget her being in this pageant. And her father would never forget the year their Christmas was stolen—and Missy got it back for them. Because one thing Missy knew: *No one* was going to steal Christmas from her and her family.

The morning had been pretty quiet. Missy was thankful.

At noon, Paul said he wanted to accompany her to her beauty pageant practice. She told him it would be nothing but listening to a bunch of instructions. Paul still insisted on going. Missy knew the real reason he was coming though: He was watching out for her. He wanted to make sure Mashela didn't show up and spoil the party.

Rapper stayed home to play with Killer until his dad came. Mr. Rapfield was supposed to arrive around 3 p.m., so Missy and Paul said their goodbyes before leaving. Missy was sad to see Rapper go, but knew he'd have a blast with his dad.

It was the afternoon of December 23 and chilly outside. The Superkids headed up the steps of the local country club. This was where the Miss Nautical Christmas Pageant would be held. Paul pulled open the big, old-fashioned door and motioned Missy inside.

The entryway sounded hollow as they walked through it. Missy and Paul had opted to take a HoverTaxi this time, so they weren't dressed to the hilt in warm gear. Missy unzipped her dark-blue winter coat—her favorite one with the blue, faux fur around the top—and approached an information desk. The clerk behind it didn't even look up. He just pointed toward "Dinner Hall B." Missy led the way.

At the door, Missy was greeted by a tall, thin woman

with diamond earrings. She asked Missy for her entry form. Missy felt her stomach grip as she handed it over. Something about it brought Missy back to her history of beauty contests. Suddenly she remembered not the glamour, but the pressure. She remembered the fierce competition between girls. She remembered putting petroleum jelly on her teeth so her lips wouldn't stick to them. Missy shivered. *That was just gross.*

Missy forced herself to focus. *Come on, it wasn't that bad, was it?* Diamond Earrings handed Missy an electronic tablet with a built-in keyboard. "Fill this out and hand it in by 1:30," she said looking at her watch. "You made it in just in time."

"Thank you."

The Superkids found a nearby bench and took a seat. Paul looked over Missy's shoulder at the questions. Periodically, a girl or two would walk by, trekking between the washroom and Dinner Hall B. Missy focused on the questionnaire and kept from comparing herself with the other contestants. She had learned early on that comparing yourself to others didn't help you win. It just heaped on a boatload of unnecessary worry.

Paul must have noticed her hesitation, because he said, "You know Proverbs 31:30 says charm is deceptive and

beauty is fleeting, but a woman who fears the Lord is to
be praised."

Missy smiled. "I know. This is just bringing back all
kinds of feelings I'd forgotten about. I'm just having to deal
with them again."

Missy filled in her name, "Missy Crystal Ashton," her
address, ComPhone number, etc., etc., etc. Then came age,
height, weight, etc., etc., etc.

Two more girls walked by. One looked down at Missy.
She quickly turned away when she made eye contact.

"I'm so glad I know Jesus," Missy said to Paul. "You
know, maybe I shouldn't do this."

Paul shrugged. "It's up to you. But don't quit because
of them."

"I know. I won't. It's just…this is so vain—everything
is—without Him."

Next came the questions that were the hardest to fill
out: the essay questions. Most didn't require more than a
sentence answer, but they were always subjective—no real
right or wrong response. The first was, *What do you want to
be when you become an adult?* Missy knew she wanted to
be a fashion designer, so that's what she entered. Having
grown up with her dad being the head of a clothing factory,
she knew a lot about clothes. Plus, she had a pretty good

fashion sense, or so she'd been told.

What three qualities do you look for in a friend?

Missy typed, "The three qualities I look for in a friend are honesty, integrity and trustworthiness."

"Is 'trustworthiness' a word?" she asked Paul.

He shrugged. "Just put 'trust.'" And she did.

If you were going to heaven tomorrow, what one thing would you take with you?

Missy smiled, "This could lead to an altar call." Then, "Geez, how do I answer that?"

"I can't answer it for you."

"Well, it's not like you can take anything with you when you go."

"How about Killer? If you went to heaven, wouldn't you want him to come along?"

"Oh pah-leeze. Just what God needs—a DobShepPoo guarding the Pearly Gates."

"Hey, I wasn't the one who had the dog in my room all night."

"What? I..." Missy pursed her lips and turned back to the questionnaire. "Quiet. I'm trying to fill this thing out."

She wrote, "If I went to heaven tomorrow, I'd want to take along the best memories of my family and friends."

"Good answer," Paul said. "*And* theologically correct."

"Hmm."

She continued down the questionnaire, providing answers about her interests, hobbies and beliefs. As she finished, Paul spoke up.

"Check this out," he said, reaching over and touching the bottom of the screen. He pointed to a block of small type. "According to this, there's going to be a talent competition, a question and answer segment and a…Santa outfit competition?"

Missy nodded. "They do it at all the Christmas pageants. We have to dress up in red Santa outfits and walk across the stage. I'll take it over a swimsuit competition any day."

"Should be interesting."

"Promises loads of holiday cheer."

"So what are you doing for the talent competition?"

"I'll sing. Not sure what yet. What I'm really concerned about is the question and answer segment. It's pretty hard to come up with a good answer on the spot, in front of everyone."

"You mean you don't know what questions they're going to ask?"

"Not exactly. Usually they base them on the answers and interests you put on this questionnaire. But there's no telling what they're going to ask you exactly. You need to be prepared for anything."

Missy tapped in the last few letters and scanned the document once more. She corrected the spelling of a couple words, then stood up.

"Here I go," she said, heading to the entrance of the auditorium. Paul was right behind her.

A sly smile crept across Mashela's face. She waited until Beauty Queen handed in her questionnaire and entered the auditorium.

Swiftly, she made her way to the door, with her own electronic questionnaire in hand. She made it to the desk where the woman with the diamond earrings sat. And—*Whoops! Did I do that?*—she bumped the table, knocking Missy's questionnaire to the floor. She graciously picked it up. With sleight of hand, she pulled the old "switcheroo" and handed her own pad to the woman, apologizing for bumping it off the table.

Then, tucking Missy's questionnaire under her arm, Mashela said, "Oh, I just need another minute with mine."

Scooting through a row of girls to get to one of the
few seats left, Missy kept asking herself, *Why am I doing
this again?*

Paul had decided to stand at the back, rather than trip
and fall over the troops.

Ignoring a few glares, Missy finally reached her seat.
She greeted the girls on either side of her. She put her coat
on the back of her chair and sat down. The flimsy, metal
chair squeaked beneath her.

Moments later, Diamond Earrings addressed the
group, thanking them "for participating in this year's
Miss Nautical Christmas Pageant." She explained that
100 girls had entered this year's contest, and as far as
she was concerned, they were all winners. Nonetheless,
only one could really win. So! Practice, practice, practice—your walk, your talent and your talk—over the next
couple of days...

Missy was familiar with this speech. It would be followed by the instructions as to where each girl would stand
and when, and where each one would walk, the order of the
pageant, and more.

But first, "OK, now let's have each young lady
stand up and give us your name, your age and a little
bit about yourself."

One by one the girls took turns sharing a tidbit
of information.

"I'm Ashley Sue from Cicero. I'm 15. My hobbies are
reading, skiing and piano."

"My name is Meagan Grant. I'm 14 years old. I like to
write poetry and listen to music."

"Belle Fuentez. Sixteen. Singing and carpentry. But
generally not at the same time."

A few minutes passed as the first row finished, then the
second. Missy was on the third, in the middle. The last girl
on row two stood.

"Missy!" The Superkid looked down at her ComWatch.
Paul was peering out at her. The girls on either side of
Missy looked over.

Missy looked at each one and smiled courteously. Then
she bowed her head and drew close to her ComWatch.

"What?" Missy whispered back. "I'm kinda busy."

"Well, I…OK, don't stress."

"What is it?"

"Well, you promise you won't stress?"

"Of course, I promise. What?"

"Well…"

"Well, what?"

"Next!"

"Huh?" Missy looked up.

Diamond Earrings had her hands on her hips. "You're next," she said.

"Oh, sorry," Missy said, flustered. She stood up and straightened her outfit. "I'm, um, Missy Crystal Ashton. I'm 13 years old." She started to sit.

Diamond: "Any hobbies, interests?"

"Oh." Missy stood up fully again. "Um, I like singing and clothing design."

Diamond nodded. Missy smiled and sat down. The girl on her right side stood and spoke. Missy returned to her ComWatch.

"Now what's so important that it couldn't wait?"

"OK, look five seats down from you."

Missy leaned forward. She couldn't see past the girl standing four chairs away.

"I can't see."

"It's—"

"Mashela Knavery," said the next participant. Missy's head shot up and she looked down the aisle, wide-eyed.

Mashela said, "I'm 14, and my hobbies include working out and"—she turned to Missy and winked—"spending quality time with my friends."

Then she sat down.

Missy felt like a tornado was blowing right through her
stomach. She sat stunned as the rest of the girls introduced
themselves. She couldn't help but sit and wonder what
Mashela was up to this time. Why had she entered the contest? Was this her way of coming out on top? Was she actually going to try and compete?

Sure, she was beautiful and could be as charming as
anyone, but...was she really entering the contest?

For Missy, the rest of the practice was just going
through the motions. She tried to listen, but her thoughts
kept straying to the girl seated only five seats away. Near
the end, Diamond Earrings walked everyone through the
stage area. Missy couldn't keep her eyes off Mashela. The
ex-NME agent wouldn't even look back. She just giggled
with the girls around her. Every once in a while, one of the
other girls would look back at Missy and suppress a laugh.
God only knew what she was telling them.

Missy didn't know why it mattered what they thought.
She didn't even know these girls. But it still hurt, thinking
Mashela was spreading lies. Missy tightened her jaw.

At the end of practice, Missy tried to brush by Mashela.
She wanted to ask her what she thought she was doing, but
Mashela avoided her. She thought about saying something
to Diamond Earrings, but how catty would that sound? *Um,*

could you disqualify her please? I have no evidence, but she broke into my house and stole all my presents. Oh, and then she tore up a small collectibles store. Yeah, guess she wasn't spending enough quality time with her friends.

Missy paged Paul on her ComWatch.

When Paul answered, Missy could tell he was moving. "I'm after her," he said quickly.

"Where are you?"

"She went out the west door. I'm about halfway down the hall."

"I'm coming."

Missy jumped off the stage. Then she faltered for a minute as she tried to figure out which direction was west. Finally, remembering where the sun was in relation to the building, she headed for a set of doors on the far side of the auditorium.

She burst through the doors and could hear running in the distance. Missy ran forward, slapping her ComWatch on the way.

"She went out a back door," Paul shouted.

"I'm right behind you!" Missy could see Paul now. He exited out the door.

"Umph!" Missy looked at her ComWatch and saw distorted images as Paul fell forward.

"Paul!" she cried.

Missy reached the door and popped it open. Paul was sitting up, rubbing his elbow.

"She tripped me," he said.

Up on a ledge, just out of reach, Mashela waved and then disappeared. Missy looked for some way to catch up with her, but she was too far ahead. Missy decided against it. She helped Paul up and he winced.

"You all right?"

"Just a bruise," he said flatly.

Suddenly a chill shot through Missy. "It's freezing out here!"

Paul agreed. Together they re-entered the building. As they made their way down the hall, Paul was quiet. Missy asked him what was wrong. Solemnly, he admitted, "I can't tell what she's going to do next."

"Well, maybe nothing," Missy said. "Nothing we can't handle with God anyway."

"I hope so," Paul replied. "Because right after she tripped me, she said she'd be visiting us tonight."

"It just doesn't make sense," Missy said, her hands wrapped around a mug of hot chocolate. "How does she know where we are? What we're doing? How did she know I was going to enter the beauty contest?"

Paul shook his head.

Killer came trotting into the kitchen and plopped down at Missy's feet. Her parents were upstairs finalizing some paperwork for the Christmas Angel dinner. Suddenly, to both Superkids' surprise, Rapper walked into the room.

"Hey, no one gonna offer me a cup?" he cracked.

Paul stood up and walked to the sink. He grabbed a cup and filled it with scorching water as Missy asked, "Rapper, what are you still doing here? Is everything all right?"

Rapper shrugged. "He just hasn't shown. I called him, but no one answered."

"He must be on his way."

Rapper accepted the cup of hot chocolate from Paul.

Missy wanted to encourage Rapper, but it was

difficult given his dad's track record. Rapper had told Missy more than once how his dad forgot things and was generally absent. It was sad, and Missy wasn't sure how to be positive about this turn of events. Surely he was coming—it was Christmas. Missy just couldn't relate. Honestly, she had "perfect" parents, if there was such a thing. Rapper had to know she had no idea what he was feeling.

"So what's up?" Rapper asked, changing the subject. "You signed up to be the beauty queen of Nautical?"

Paul's eyebrows shot up. "But now she has serious competition."

"You think Mashela's serious competition?" Missy asked.

"No—I just—"

"Mashela's in the contest?" Rapper clued in.

Paul and Missy nodded.

"But she's not serious competition," Missy countered.

"I need to start going with you two more," Rapper stated. "I'm missing out on all the good stuff. So what—did she follow you there?"

"No, that's what's strange. It's like she knew we were going there."

Paul added, "I don't know how, but it's like she can hear *everything* we say."

In an instant, Rapper turned white. Missy and Paul didn't miss it.

"What?" they both said in unison.

"She *can* hear everything you say," Rapper whispered.

"How?" Missy said cautiously.

Rapper pointed at Missy and Paul's wrists. "Your ComWatches."

Paul was doubtful. "It's a secure frequency. Even NME hasn't been able to tap into it."

"She doesn't *need* to tap into it," Rapper explained. He pulled up his left sleeve. "She stole my ComWatch before she dropped me off in the junkyard last month—remember? All she has to do is tune in to hear everything you two say. Good thing my new one hasn't been issued yet."

"It's not that easy," Missy said, quickly removing her ComWatch. Paul took his off, too. "I'd have to let *her* listen—and she'd have to be within a couple of miles at all times."

"We've thought she was close. And to tune in, all she has to do is call you up."

Paul and Missy were looking closely at their ComWatches, pushing the buttons. "But wouldn't we hear her?" Missy asked.

Pow! Suddenly Mashela's face appeared on both

Superkids' ComWatches. They jolted back and dropped the devices. "C'mon, haven't you ever turned your ComWatch all the way down and called someone with a whisper? Oh, that's right: You did it just last month when you were searching for me in Superkid Academy. You know, if you darken the display, too, the other person won't even know you're there!"

Missy's mouth went dry. Paul squeezed his eyes shut. How could they have overlooked this?

Missy stared at Mashela in the ComWatch screen. "You've been listening in on *everything,* haven't you? And this is how I've heard your voice in my room every night. You just spoke through my ComWatch."

"Brilliant deduction, Tootle."

Missy's eyes hardened on Mashela's face. "I'm so glad you entered that contest," Missy said, angry.

"Oh, I don't know. I hear I'm pretty serious competition."

"You think you can steal my Christmas? You can't. *You can't!* I'm going to win that contest and win back seven times what you've stolen from me!"

"Well, you'd better win then. Because if I win, I'll have stolen your Christmas *twice.*"

Missy slammed a button on top of her ComWatch hard with her fingertips, shutting down the transmission. She snatched Paul's watch, too, and shut it down. Then, in one swift motion, she threw the watches across the room. They slammed into the wall and fell to the floor. Paul and Rapper looked at each other in surprise. Killer jumped up and walked over to smell the watches.

Softly, Paul said, "She's just a bunch of talk."

"She's not just a bunch of talk!" Missy shouted, jumping up. Her chair shrieked as it scooted back. "She's been following me, trying to hurt me! She broke into my house and took away our security—she even broke into my *bedroom*. Why is she doing this? Doesn't she have anything better to do?!!"

Missy's voice hung in the air. The boys stayed quiet and Missy let out a long breath.

"I'm—I'm sorry. You guys don't deserve the wrath of Missy. She's just...really got me on edge. I've never had to face this before. Not like this."

"I hate persecution," Rapper said, speaking from experience. "I have to force myself to remember Matthew 5:11-12. It says we should be glad when people insult us, say untrue things about us and persecute us. Because then we know we'll have a great reward in heaven. I say it's a way you can know you're living for God—like the Christians who lived long ago."

Missy plopped back down in her chair, but didn't bother to pull it up to the table. "Well at least I'm past the crying stage. Now I'm just angry."

Paul looked back over his shoulder at Killer licking the watches. "You've got quite an arm there, Slugger."

▲   ▲   ▲

Half an hour later, the hot chocolate was cold and Missy picked up the mugs. She placed them in the dishwasher and closed the door. A couple of minutes later, they were clean and dry. She put them back in the cupboard.

The doorbell chimed and Rapper's eyes lit up. "Yes! Finally," he said. He jumped up and took off toward the front door.

When he was out of the room, Paul looked at Missy and said, "Thank God. I'm so glad he showed. I was starting to wonder."

Missy nodded. "Me too. It's got to be hard for Rapper. Doesn't help that everything is so stressful here."

Paul raised his eyebrows. "I'll give him a hand. You can feed Killer."

"Gee thanks."

Paul left the room. Missy let out a long breath. Killer's head popped up.

"He was just kidding," Missy assured the DobShepPoo. "Your dinner isn't for another couple of hours."

The dog whimpered and set his head back down.

Missy heard her friends' voices outside and she looked at Killer. "Well, I guess it's time to meet the infamous Mr. Rapfield."

As she walked out of the kitchen, Missy patted her pant leg, beckoning Killer to join her. The dog jumped up and followed her.

Missy could feel the cold air blowing in. *Why didn't they close the door?* she wondered.

Behind her, Killer stopped in his tracks and his ears drew back.

Missy walked through the door. She walked onto the wide porch—six white pillars around her, set in marble. It was eerily quiet. She folded her arms together for warmth. She could see her breath in the air. Killer stepped behind her.

"Paul?!" she shouted. "Rapper?!"

A low, growling sound came from Killer's throat. Missy started to turn, then she saw Paul and Rapper—both lying in a thin layer of snow, looking dazed.

Missy started toward them when suddenly—*FWOOM!*— Mashela's face appeared in front of hers—upside-down.

"Déjà vu, again," she said and—*WHUMP!*—she punched Missy in the face.

Missy shrieked and stumbled back. Killer yelped as she landed on his paw. He retreated backward through the open door, trying to avoid her. Missy lost her footing and smashed into the door frame, her shoulder blade hitting the door button. *SHOOOM!* The door closed quickly, shutting Killer inside.

"Woof! Woof! Woof!" Killer barked, furiously.

"Didn't expect that, did ya?" Mashela asked, dropping down to the ground. "See, I'm not all beauty. Brains too." She winked.

"What are you doing?!" Missy cried, holding her burning eye.

"Just here to knock out the competition."

"Ugh!" Missy shouted. With full force, she charged forward.

Mashela, clearly taken by surprise, whirled around and ran off the porch. Paul and Rapper, who had just stood up, were both knocked to the ground as she plowed by. Missy leapt over them and caught Mashela's backpack. She threw her weight around and tossed her right leg under Mashela's. The ex-NME agent slipped and fell as Missy tackled her and shoved her to the ground.

"Where did you learn how to do that?!" Mashela cried between breaths.

"I'm highly trained, too—we're the same, remember?"

Killer barked and barked from inside the house.

Mashela rolled over, pulling Missy along with her. The girls rolled sideways and—*Kerthump!*—right into a snowdrift inside a fountain bed. Snow fell upon them, hitting Missy in the face. Missy could feel the cold press against her back. She kicked and threw her power from her elbows.

With the advantage, Mashela jumped up and threw down a fast punch. Missy, though aching, was quick. She rolled to the side, avoiding the blow. Mashela's hand hit the snow.

Missy flipped up into a horse-riding stance. She stood ready. Behind Mashela, she could see Rapper helping Paul up.

Suddenly Missy's parents appeared at the door. Mashela wasn't even phased at hearing Mr. Ashton mispronounce her name. But she did hear the door open. And she heard Killer barking as he shot across the porch.

She asked Missy, "How 'bout now? Love me any less?"

"What? I—no."

But Mashela was gone. She tore down the Ashtons'

wide front lawn, closely tailed by Missy's angry, barking DobShepPoo.

Missy watched as they rounded the corner and flew out of sight.

"Catch her!" Mr. Ashton cheered after Killer. He and his wife were now near Missy. Mrs. Ashton grabbed Missy's hand and looked at her swelling eye. Paul and Rapper joined them.

Then everyone stood silently and turned to the corner hedge, waiting to see what happened.

And they waited.

And they listened.

And when they heard and saw nothing, they waited some more.

Then Paul said, "You think he got her?"

To which Rapper replied, "I think she knocked him out."

Then Killer appeared. Standing tall, standing strong. Wagging his tail. Holding something thick and wide in his mouth.

Everyone strained to see what it was.

Missy called to Killer and he drew closer.

She retracted. "Eww. What is that?"

Paul peered closer. "Is it some kind of animal?"

Rapper chimed in, "That's not Mashela's foot, is it?"

"OK!" Missy said turning. "I'm grossed out."

Killer finally reached them and proudly dropped the item at their feet. He barked.

"Well, you could say it's an animal," Mr. Ashton announced as he bent down. "Or, at least, it used to be." He picked it up with two fingers. Missy turned around and looked.

Mr. Ashton said, "It's a partially frozen…um…T-bone steak."

Killer barked.

"She really does come prepared, doesn't she?" said Rapper.

Paul petted Killer. "The way to a dog's heart is through his stomach."

Missy just shook her head. She grabbed the steak, put it on her swollen eye and marched into the house.

Killer was right behind her.

It was 2 a.m., the night before the pageant and Missy couldn't sleep. She wasn't sure why, exactly. She felt safe in her room with Killer at her feet. With the ComWatch trick figured out, she didn't have to wonder if Mashela was in her room anymore. Her dad had beefed up their security system to the latest and greatest so they wouldn't have to be on guard. And, on top of that, since Mashela was entering the beauty pageant, Missy figured she'd be getting a good night's sleep, too, if she were smart. And she was.

Missy tapped on the light. She sat up in bed, cross-legged, and petted Killer. "Boy, you'd better not have fleas," she said with a yawn. She winced. Her eye still hurt. She felt like a cement truck had run over her. She had a thin layer of healing medicine covering her eye, and when she looked in the mirror, it looked really bad. Really bad. All red and black and blue and gross. The judges would love that.

Missy got out of bed and threw on her robe. She didn't bother brushing her tangled, blond hair. Instead, she just grabbed the cold pack by her headboard, held it to her eye and went downstairs for a middle-of-the-night orange juice.

The kitchen tile was cool on her feet. She was filling up her glass when she noticed light coming from the living room. Since Killer was calm, she knew nothing was wrong. She poured a second glass and walked to the living room, balancing the cold pack on her head.

She stopped in the entryway when she spied Rapper sitting there, on the sofa, staring at the twinkling Christmas tree.

"Hey," she said.

Rapper turned and smiled. "Hey."

"Couldn't sleep?"

"Nope."

"Me neither. Here."

Rapper took the orange juice from her. She removed the cold pack from her head.

"Thanks," he said. "Nice hair."

Missy rolled her eyes up and looked at her blond bangs. She could only imagine how twisty and curly her hair was at this hour. "It's a new look for me. Au natural."

She sat down in her dad's comfy recliner. She put the cold pack to her eye. Killer sat on the floor at her side.

The Christmas tree, reprogrammed by her mother, was

still pretty—even without presents surrounding its base. The lights twinkled throughout, a star twinkled on top. The tabletop, marble Nativity scene still sat beside it, giving Missy a warm feeling.

"Still waiting for your dad?"

"Yeah."

"Mmm."

"Well, I would be *if* I thought he was really gonna come."

"I'm sorry," Missy said.

Rapper let out a long breath. "I finally got hold of him."

Missy raised her eyebrows. It hurt.

"Yeah, he got tied up at work. Decided to wait another day. Didn't bother to call and let me know, though."

"Ouch."

"Mmm."

"You blame him?"

Rapper shook his head. "No. I mean, it's no excuse, but he doesn't know the Lord. Until he makes Jesus the Lord of His life, he's not going to be the man of God he could be. I'm praying for him, and believing. But at times like this, it's not easy."

"You want to fly home to your mom's for Christmas? I'm sure Daddy will help out in any way he can."

"No—it's all right. He'll be coming. He's just late. But

is it all right if I stay here a little longer?"

"Of course. Hey, the Blue Squad sticks together."

"Definitely." Then Rapper changed the subject. "Hey, I'm sorry for all this trouble with Mashela."

Missy giggled. "It's not your fault."

"Well, I can't help but wonder if she found you because she followed me. I mean, last time we saw her, she kidnapped me. Maybe she's been watching me since then."

Missy set her drink on a coaster on the table beside her. "She's been watching us all. Believe me, this time it's personal with Mashela. It's all about me. She's testing me. And she's not going to win."

"You sound like her."

"In some ways we're the same."

"I highly doubt that."

"Well, we're both stubborn, that's for sure." Missy laughed and then winced. She pulled the cold pack off her eye and asked Rapper, "How bad is it?"

"What?" Rapper asked.

"Very funny. Hey! You'll get to stay for the beauty pageant tomorrow."

"Wow. You really are stubborn," Rapper said. "Most girls would give up after getting a black eye."

"I'm not most girls."

"No argument there."

A few moments later, Missy added, "But I shouldn't have knocked her down."

"When?"

"When she punched me earlier today. I didn't exactly turn the other cheek. I launched out at her."

"She was attacking you."

"I know. But…I went past the point of protecting myself. For a second there, I felt like I wanted to hurt her for what she was doing. Give her a black eye back."

"But you didn't hurt her."

"No."

Missy picked up her orange juice again and savored a swallow. She followed up by saying, "Persecution is a strange thing."

"How so?"

"Well, I don't think there's always a reason behind it. I mean, I know Mashela's wanting to prove me wrong. Prove that I don't love her. Teach me something. But she's going to extremes to do it. And she flat out admits she's doing it just because I'm a Christian. And to make it stranger, we pray for God's protection, but I still end up with a black eye."

"You know, we're in the same kind of situation," Rapper noted.

Missy waited for him to continue. He said, "Mashela's beating up on you. My dad doesn't show up. In both cases, God won't force them to do the right thing. They have to live with their actions."

"But their actions affect us."

"Which opens the door for God to move," Rapper said. "Someone once told me your Christmas can only be stolen if you let it be stolen."

He stood up and walked over to Missy. Then he placed his hand over her eye. "God, right now in the Name of Jesus, I pray that You would heal Missy's eye completely and entirely. First Peter 2:24 says You bore this pain on the cross. Take this pain away from Missy, I pray. Show her how to handle Mashela as You call out to Mashela's heart. Touch her life like she's never been touched before. In Jesus' Name. Amen."

When he pulled away, Missy kept her eyes closed, adding, "And Father, I agree with Rapper that his dad discovers a new life in You. Like Matthew 9:38 says, we pray that the right people come across his path at the right time—so You can change him from the inside out."

"Thanks," Rapper said. Then he yawned. "Well, I'm going to hit the sack. You should, too. You have a big day tomorrow."

Slurp! Missy quickly pulled her feet under her as Killer laid a big, sloppy kiss on her toes.

"Gross!" she cried.

Rapper laughed. "So have you come up with a new name for Killer yet?"

"Not yet," Missy said, pushing the DobShepPoo away.

"So are you leaning toward a name that reflects his sweet side or his rough and gruff?"

"Rough and gruff? For this big baby?" Missy asked.

Rapper shrugged. Killer's eyes blinked.

"Maybe I'll name him Mashela," Missy quipped.

▲　　▲　　▲

Missy was the last one to Christmas Eve brunch. She came in with wet hair, but with a smile on her face. Of course, it was hard not to smile when her mother greeted her singing, "Merry Christmas E-eve!"

Missy had another reason to smile, too. Her mother noticed it first. "Tootle! Your black eye is going away! Praise the Lord!" And it was true. After Rapper's prayer, it had started healing quickly—and it looked better every time Missy passed a mirror.

"Rad," Rapper said.

Over a brunch of pancakes, eggs, toast and sausage,

Mrs. Ashton was the first to bring up the previous day's encounter again.

"Tootle…Is Superkid Academy always this dangerous?"

Missy smiled. Her mom was always looking out for her. "The world is dangerous, now," she said. "But at Superkid Academy, they teach us how to live in victory by putting our trust and faith in God. And they teach us how to live by His Word and overcome the enemy."

Mr. Ashton added, "It just concerns us. All you kids facing other kids like this Mush-ela."

"Muh-*shay*-la, Daddy."

"Isn't that what I said? Anyway, I've decided that until this all cools down, I'm going to hire a security team to watch over you. Especially through the beauty contest."

"Daddy—that's really not necessary. That's why we got Killer."

"Killer," Gregg Ashton said, pointing his fork at the dog, "can be bought off with a T-bone steak. I'm taking him back."

Killer's head popped up. "Rrrr?"

Missy was shocked. "Daddy, no. I like Killer."

"I thought you couldn't stand him."

"Well…he's…growing on me. I just need to change his name."

"But, Tootle, you're only home on vacations."

Mrs. Ashton jumped in, "Well, we should keep him for when Tootle comes home." Missy smiled. Her mom was liking the mutt, too.

"Well, regardless," Mr. Ashton said, "I'm getting security. They'll be here in a few hours."

Missy could just imagine a SWAT team escorting her around the stage.

"Daddy, really. It's no big deal. I can handle it."

"Missy," Mr. Ashton said, in a familiar tone. It was the tone that said, "Don't argue with me on this. My decision is final."

Missy gave in.

Her mom encouraged, "It's for your protection."

Missy nodded.

"I'm getting a couple guys to watch the house while we're out too. It'd be just like this Mush-ela girl to try and break into our safe on Christmas Eve. And all our presents are in there."

"I guess it is a good idea," Missy conceded.

Then Lois Ashton turned to Rapper. "Did your parents ever call?"

Rapper nodded. "Yeah, I got ahold of my dad. He's coming late tonight, I think. Is it all right if I stay—"

"Of course," Mrs. Ashton said looking at her husband. He winked at her.

Missy said, "Well, this is going to be one full day. The pageant's only about nine hours away. I still need to get a few outfits together, practice my walk, speaking...ugh."

Mrs. Ashton squeezed Missy's arm. "I'm so excited!"

Mr. Ashton squeezed her shoulder. "You're going to do great. I was able to get front row seats for all of us."

"Really?" Paul said. "Great!"

"I'll do my best," Missy stated.

"That's all we want," Mr. Ashton assured her.

"So what's the competition like?" Rapper asked.

"It's serious," Missy admitted, looking at Paul. He grinned.

"She's never lost a title yet," Mrs. Ashton chimed in. "One year, a certain contest chairperson—who shall remain nameless—actually asked us *not* to enter Missy. He said he wanted to give the other girls a chance."

"She's just kidding," Missy said to Paul and Rapper.

"I'm totally serious," Mrs. Ashton corrected.

"Really?" Paul asked.

"Really?" Rapper asked.

"All those contests she's won, and I've never even had to bribe the judges."

"Daddy! Like you would."

Mr. Ashton got a good laugh out of that one.

"Even with a black eye, you'd give them a run," Mrs. Ashton said to her daughter.

Rapper clapped his hands together. "Well then, let's get ready. Let's go win a contest!"

As the Ashtons pulled up in their hovercar, Missy peeked in the rearview mirror and looked at her eye. It was nearly completely healed. The swelling was gone, and what color was left was easily covered by makeup.

Mr. Ashton pulled up at the back of the country club, at the contestant entrance. Other families were dropping their daughters off, too. Missy took a deep breath and popped open the door. Her mother gave her a final cheer. Missy waved "goodbye for now" to Paul and Rapper. Her dad exited with her. He popped open the trunk with a button on his key chain.

Missy pulled out her makeup bag and four changes of clothes. Her dad kissed her on the forehead. "You'll do great. I'm very proud of you."

"I haven't won yet, Daddy."

"That doesn't change anything."

Missy walked onto the curb when Paul jumped out of the car.

"Hey, why don't I come with you," he said.

Missy looked at the girls entering the building. "You

want to come with me into a room full of primping girls?"

Paul thought about it a second. "Um. Come to think of it, no. I'll meet you later."

Missy laughed. "Thanks anyway."

Mr. Ashton and Paul entered the hovercar. Suddenly, behind them, the doors opened on a small, sleek, black hovercar. Two men in black jumped out, then stood perfectly still, staring at Missy. One was tall and slender, with a long face and black hair combed straight back. The other was his twin...except short and stubby, with a wart on either side of his nose.

Missy knocked on her dad's window. He zipped it down.

"Daddy, do Geek and Eek have to follow me everywhere I go?"

"They're here for your protection. They'll keep you safe."

Missy smiled. "OK, Daddy. Just checkin'."

Mr. Ashton drove off. Geek and Eek didn't move a hair.

Missy shook her head and took a step toward the back door.

Geek and Eek took a step toward the back door.

Missy stopped.

Geek and Eek stopped.

Missy took another step toward the back door.

Geek and Eek took another step.

Missy stopped.

Geek and Eek stopped.

Missy spun around. "Do you guys think maybe you can be a little less obvious?"

Geek and Eek looked at each other. They looked back at her and at the same time asked, "What?"

It was going to be a long night.

Missy entered the building, leaving Geek and Eek outside without a backstage pass. The last thing she needed was for them to be inside, helping her apply makeup. Instead, they would guard the back door like seasoned professionals. She had no problem waving goodbye. They seemed unsure about waving back.

The large dressing room had thin, rosy carpeting on the floor and a high ceiling. It was lined with small vanity tables, each one displaying a mirror circled in light. The room was abuzz with sound as a hundred contestants prepared for the big night. Designated helpers with Christmas tree badges fluttered around the room, taking care of last-minute needs.

One named Candy rushed up and handed Missy a photocopied map. Missy located her vanity table—#74—and made

her way toward it. On her way, she passed girls of all back-
grounds and nationalities, each more beautiful than the last.
The feeling came back—that feeling of competition, of vanity,
of stress. And with it came a sadness. Missy knew many of
these girls weren't Christians. They didn't know how tempo-
rary outside beauty was. They didn't know there was a better
way, a higher way, a freer way. These girls were Missy's min-
istry. She longed to do the best she could, being a good example of Christ to them. Like 1 Timothy 4:12 said, she wanted to
be an example in speech, in life, in love, in faith and in purity.
"Lord, I'll need Your help," she whispered.

Missy slowed her walk as she realized many of the girls
were turning away quickly when they saw her coming. She
heard a couple suppress snickers. Two girls whispered to
each other just after she passed them. Missy felt something
arise within her—a feeling bordering on anger and embarrassment. She had no doubt what the snickering was about.
It could be summed up in one word: Mashela. Missy didn't
even want to know what rumors she'd spread.

After a walk that seemed an eternity, Missy reached
vanity table #74. She hung her outfits on a protruding steel
bar. She said hello to the girls on either side of her. They
mumbled hello as she sat down.

Missy looked at her eye in the well-lit mirror. It actually

looked great. Mashela's plan to "knock Missy out" of the race didn't work.

The girl on Missy's right was applying her makeup. She kept glancing over. But Missy didn't pay any attention to her. She didn't want to start worrying. She didn't want to wonder what everyone else was thinking…what everyone else had been told. She told herself she just needed to rejoice amidst the persecution. Her reward in heaven would be great because of it.

Missy looked at the map of the room again. On the back, she located Mashela's name. Vanity table #31. Missy oriented herself and looked behind her. There she was. Mashela was applying makeup to her face, laughing with the girl beside her. As Missy watched, she let her anger and embarrassment dissolve into compassion. Mashela was so deceived. And it made Missy sad. She had so much potential. So much she could do for God. So much she may never discover if her heart stayed hardened and her eyes closed.

But she was beautiful. She would give Missy and the other girls quite a challenge.

Missy spent about 20 minutes fixing herself up. She sorted through the outfits she'd brought and found her evening dress. This was the first dress the girls had to wear onstage, as they were introduced. Next would come the

Santa outfit, then another dress for the talent contest and another for the ending.

Her evening dress was a deep, forest green, with deep red and white accents. It would have looked a little corny any other time of year, but Missy knew that at Christmastime, it was striking. She pulled the hanger away from the group and walked to the changing rooms—just down a row and to the right, according to the map. She would finish her makeup and hair after she was dressed.

Within five minutes, she had changed and was outside the rooms, looking at herself in the mirrors. Two other girls were near, doing the same thing. Missy turned around slowly, giving herself a "spot-check" from all sides.

Suddenly, she caught the girl beside her staring.

"Hi," Missy greeted her.

The girl just turned away. "Oh—I'm sorry. I don't mean to stare."

Missy's hand immediately went to her eye. "Can you really see it?" she asked.

"Oh no," the girl replied. "It's practically gone."

Missy smiled.

"I'm just surprised."

Missy stopped smiling. "Why is that?"

"Well...I heard how you got it. I'm surprised it's healed up so fast."

Missy tipped up on her toes and located Mashela, still putting on makeup. "You heard how I got this?" she asked.

The girl nodded.

"What did you hear?"

"You know—you were visiting Santa at the mall and when he wouldn't promise to give you everything you asked for, you pulled his beard."

"So you heard I pulled Santa's beard and he punched me?"

"Oh no!" the girl exclaimed. "I know Santa wouldn't do that. I heard it was one of his elves that beat you up."

Missy's mouth dropped. "You have got to be kidding me."

"Oh—I promise not to tell anyone else."

"Who have you told?"

"Just five of my friends. But don't worry. It was old news to them anyway." And with that, the girl squeezed Missy's arm and waltzed away.

Missy heard snickering behind her. She turned around. The two girls dropped their smiles immediately.

"What?" Missy asked.

"Well, I don't mean to be catty," the first said, "but we

find it hard to believe your wig looks so good. Where *did* you get it?"

"My *wig?!*"

"Yeah, we heard that—"

Missy grabbed a clump of her golden hair. "This is the real thing, baby. Homegrown and—who told you that?"

The girls shrugged. "Just heard it around. Don't take it personal. It really does look real." They walked away.

Missy could feel her blood beginning to boil. She marched down the aisle. *Whatever,* she thought. *I'll just go back to my seat and forget they even—*

"I hope you don't win."

Missy stopped in her tracks and spun around. A cute little redhead was glaring at her.

"What did you say?" Missy asked.

"I said I hope you don't win. Just because your dad is rich doesn't mean you have the right to bribe all the judges with gifts."

"What?!"

"You heard me. How tacky." The girl retreated.

Missy couldn't believe it. First Mashela was messing with Missy. Then Paul and Rapper. Then her family. Now with other people!

Missy grabbed the nearest chair and jumped on top of

it. Then she leapt onto vanity table #56. Her wide, green Christmas dress pressed against the mirror.

"May I have your attention, please?!" Missy shouted. She looked over and saw Mashela grin. Then she disappeared behind her mirror. Missy was hot. "May I have your attention?!" The room fell instantly silent. "I want you all to know you've been manipulated and fed lies about me!"

A couple rows away, a girl said, "I heard she had a temper."

"I do *not* have a temp—" Missy lowered her voice. "I do not have a temper." Her lips were tight. "I just want you to know—"

Another girl cried out, "So it's not true that you set a bomb off in a downtown building last year?"

Missy stumbled in her words. "Well, I…I was there, but—"

"I heard your parents call you Tootle because—"

"Watch it!" Missy warned, pointing at another girl.

A fourth announced, "I heard you were a spoiled, rich girl and you think the world revolves around you."

"That is *not* true! I am *not* spoiled!"

"Yeah—and I heard you had personal servants, and personal drivers and personal bodyguards!"

"I do not have servants and drivers and GUARDS!" Missy cried.

BOOM! Suddenly the back door burst open. Geek and Eek rushed into the room, drawing their weapons and shouting, "DOWN! EVERYBODY DOWN!"

Whoomp! Like lightning, all the girls but Missy hit the floor, belly first.

Missy's mouth went dry and her voice escaped her. "I—I—don't even know them!"

Geek asked, "Is everything all right, Miss Ashton?"

Missy bit her upper lip and quickly nodded. "Yeah, yeah. You can go. Really. Please."

Geek and Eek withdrew their weapons and placed them back inside their long coats. They looked around the room one last time, then swiftly exited.

Missy looked around at all the girls staring up at her. "Um, I'm—I'm sorry. What I meant to say was that I don't *normally* have guards…um…I'm just going to go back to my table now. Um…sorry."

Quickly, Missy stepped down and made her way back to her seat.

This certainly wasn't turning out to be the Christmas Eve she had hoped for.

Across the room, Mashela peered around her mirror

again. She mouthed the question, "Love me?"

▲　　▲　　▲

Missy, feeling completely humiliated, decided to stay quiet. *Don't think about it. Don't think about it,* she kept saying to herself.

She finished getting ready, ignoring stares and whispers. And soon she fell into line with the other girls, ready to go onstage. She was number 74 corresponding with her vanity table number. She was glad they weren't in alphabetical order. If they had been, she would have been one of the first girls onstage. From experience, she knew it was best *not* to be first—because then you'd be easier to forget.

Missy looked back and saw Mashela coming. She was going onstage before Missy. The Superkid decided to ignore her. Better that than to completely lash out. This was one of those times she really wanted to show her love with her fists. She straightened her dress and rocked on her heels.

Mashela walked by, without glancing over. But she did whisper, "Break a leg," as she passed.

Five minutes passed before the fanfare started and the audience clapped. It sounded like a full room. She heard Diamond Earrings talking to the crowd. Another round of clapping and the music again. Then, the curtain to the stage was drawn back and the first girl walked out. Music played, the audience clapped and cameras flashed. One by one, the girls took their turn in the spotlight, ending their walk by standing at the back of the stage, where they would stay throughout the segment.

Missy took three deep breaths. She wasn't sure why, but her stomach was in knots. It had been awhile since she'd done this.

"Mashela Knavery."

Missy looked up and watched Mashela disappear onto the stage. She heard several "Ooos" and "Aahs," which didn't make it any easier.

"Hey, you all right?"

Missy turned and was surprised to see Paul standing beside her.

"Paul! What are you doing here?"

"I miss not having our ComWatches," he said. "Just came to check up on you."

"I'm fine," she said, hoping she was right. "A little stressed."

"Has Mashela bothered you?"

"Not directly," Missy said truthfully.

Paul looked at her feet. She was still twisting on her heels. "You nervous?"

"Just…Yeah."

As the line scooted forward, they moved up together.

"You really don't have to worry," Paul promised. "Remember—you've never lost before."

"My mom didn't tell you about the Crummy Cookie Beauty Contest."

"When was this?"

Missy looked at Paul. "I was 1½? I was a bald baby. The judges weren't amused. I didn't even place."

Paul laughed. "Well, you won't have any problem tonight. You've got plenty of hair now."

"Does it look like a wig?"

"What?"

"Never mind. I'm just…do you think Mashela's really serious competition? I mean—she has a chance at beating me, doesn't she?"

"You need some serious competition," Paul returned.

"All these girls think I'm a witch," Missy protested.

"What happened?" Paul asked. They were still moving forward, getting closer to Missy's time to go out.

"I'll tell you later."

"You sure?"

"Yeah—really, it's no big deal."

"Hey, that reminds me! I read a verse this morning I

wanted to tell you about: 2 Timothy 3:11. The Apostle Paul is talking about all his persecutions and he says, 'The Lord rescued me from *all* of them.' Missy, if God did that for him, He'll do it for you."

Missy leaned over and gave Paul a hug. "Thank you," she said.

"No problem. Oh—and hey! Rapper's dad showed up!"

The surprise on Missy's face was evident. "Really?"

"Really! Rapper is pretty excited, I can tell."

Missy melted. "Oh, I'm so happy. Thank God!"

"No kidding. Thank God."

"You know, after Rapper prayed for my eye last night, I prayed that his dad would come to his senses. This is an answer to that prayer."

"No doubt. God always comes through."

"The only other thing we prayed for was a change of heart for Mashela."

Paul looked at the advancing curtain. "I believe *that's* coming, too. Don't you?"

Missy started to answer, but couldn't finish. For she was suddenly shoved onstage as the announcer shouted, "Missy Crystal Ashton!"

Missy squinted as the bright stage lights pierced her eyes. She threw on a big smile, even though her eyes hadn't yet adjusted. She was used to this happening—especially if she wasn't ready. Big orchestra music burst from large speakers and the audience applauded her.

As Missy regained her vision, she followed the predetermined line out to center stage. She walked slowly and comfortably, with a slight swing in her step. Her dress sparkled under the lights—just the effect she'd wanted.

When she reached center stage, she paused and waved and turned around. She thought she could see her parents, but wasn't sure with the lights in her eyes. She could, however, see the judges to her right, seated below stage. They were nodding, which was good.

Diamond Earrings was saying, "Missy Crystal Ashton is 13 years old and was born right here in Nautical. Currently, she receives her schooling at Superkid Academy."

Missy turned on her heel, to take her place with the rest of the girls.

Crack! Snap! The heel on Missy's right shoe popped from the stress. It shot off like a bullet and smacked one of the judges right in the arm. Pure shock replaced Missy's smile and she nearly crumpled to the ground. But she caught herself and balanced her body, putting more weight on her right toe. In a quick recovery, she flashed her smile back at the audience and curtsied. The audience laughed nervously, convinced it was all part of Missy's entrance. She looked over and saw the judge rubbing his arm, but he was smiling and showing the heel to the judge beside him. Missy finished her turn and took her place among the other girls. She ignored their stares.

Twenty-six more girls entered and joined the group, until the segment was over. It was all Missy could do to stand straight on one heel and one toe. But finally the curtains closed and the girls shuffled off. Mashela passed Missy on the way out and whispered, "Break a leg."

Missy grabbed Mashela's arm as her mouth dropped. "Did you have something to do with that?"

Mashela played innocent. "What? Me?"

Diamond Earrings intercepted them. Missy pulled off her broken shoe and looked at the heel. She couldn't tell. It could have been weakened by a cut, but there was no way to prove it.

"She's accusing me of breaking her heel," Mashela whined to Diamond Earrings.

Missy waved it off. "I'm not accusing anyone," she said.

Diamond Earrings looked down at her. "Let's keep it that way, girls." And she walked off.

Mashela looked hard at Missy and then walked away. Missy smiled. The contest was on. She couldn't let Mashela get to her now. And so far, whether Mashela had done anything or not, Missy thought her stage presence was still good. She'd be watching her back, but she was ready for more.

▲　▲　▲

Changing into Santa outfits took the girls a few minutes. Meanwhile, onstage, a trio sang "The First Noel" followed by "We Three Kings." When Missy saw Mashela retreat to the restroom, she knew it was now or never.

Missy grabbed her Santa Claus outfit and shook it out. She rushed to Mashela's vanity table and located her Santa costume. A second later, she had the costumes switched. She made sure the rack looked the same as when she had arrived—and then she shot back to her own vanity table. She waited. When Mashela came out of the bathroom, Missy entered the changing room. She put on the costume.

It fit perfectly. Even the hat looked cute on her. She pulled her hair into pigtails and it looked even cuter. She pulled on the pair of shiny, black boots. Perfect.

When she exited the changing room, Mashela was standing there, glaring at her. She was holding the other Santa outfit on a hanger.

"How did you know I'd switched them?" Mashela demanded.

Missy chuckled. "Well, I remembered the sweet holographic message you'd left us. In it, you were wearing the frumpiest Santa costume I've ever seen. I figured, given the chance, you'd try to switch it for mine."

Mashela was surprised and silent.

"Not all beauty—brains, too," Missy said. Then, "I'm sure you'll earn big points in it. I just thought it better we each wear the one we'd brought." And she walked away.

Mashela was left tapping her foot and huffing.

The Santa outfit competition went off without a hitch, but Missy did feel a little bad for Mashela. She looked ridiculous in her frumpy costume. But somehow, she still made it look adorable, like a child playing dress up.

Up next was the talent competition. This, in Missy's

opinion, was one of the most important competitions of the evening. Well, this and the Question and Answer portion.

After changing into the proper attire, each girl put herself in her own world, practicing her talent with no regard to others around. Some, like Missy, warmed themselves up by practicing musical scales with their voices. Others practiced dancing moves. Others practiced sleight of hand with top hats and bunnies. Others practiced twirling batons or juggling balls. Missy looked back at Mashela several times. She just sat in her chair, not practicing anything. She just stared—serious as anything—at a small, electronic notepad.

Quite some time passed until Missy heard Mashela's name called. As she left the room, Missy decided to follow. She knew Mashela was talented, but more at thievery and trickery. And how could anyone show those onstage?

Missy stopped in her tracks at the entrance to backstage when she saw Mashela wasn't onstage yet. Missy peeked around the corner and waited and watched. Mashela was standing at the curtain, looking out at the ballet-dancing act before her. She wore a simple, black leotard and tights. Her hands and feet were bare. Her hair was pulled back in a ponytail, bobbing just above her neck. She had the electronic pad at her side. And her knees were shaking. Missy was struck aback. *Her knees were shaking.* Could it be? A

little bit of nervousness from Mashela? Was she actually—
for once—unsure of herself? Now Missy *had* to see what
talent she was going to share.

Moments later, the audience broke into applause. The
ballet dancer exited backstage and passed Mashela, then
Missy. She recognized her—she was the one who said she
heard Missy had a temper. *Why,* Missy wondered, *do people
listen to gossip?* And worse, *why do people believe it?*

Onstage, Diamond Earrings announced Mashela's
name and after a deep breath, Mashela walked out onstage.
Missy quickly scooted around the corner and peered out
the curtain.

Mashela timidly stepped up to the microphone. Missy
wondered if she'd lose points for her poise. She bent it
down a hair, then pushed it a tad lower. When it was right
in front of her lips, she lifted her electronic pad.

The audience watched with anticipation.

Mashela said, "I'll be reading a sonnet. This is Sonnet
No. 29. By William Shakespeare."

Missy squinted. *Mashela reads Shakespeare?*

"I read it for my parents, whom I don't know very well,
and...whom I miss. Especially around this time of year."

Missy felt her heart pained inside her chest. Mashela,
even in all her troublemaking, even in all her craftiness, was

still a person. A person in need of hope, of love, of Jesus.

"Sonnet 29," Mashela began. Then, slowly, she read:

When, in disgrace with fortune and men's eyes,
I all alone beweep my outcast state
And trouble deaf heaven with my bootless cries
And look upon myself and curse my fate,

She paused and swallowed. Then continued:

Wishing me like to one more rich in hope,
Featured like him, like him with friends possess'd,
Desiring this man's art and that man's scope,
With what I most enjoy contented least;

Mashela paused again, this time looking up into the audience. It was hard to see, but Missy thought her eyes seemed glassy. The last time she'd seen Mashela express this much emotion was when she had faced her on the rooftop of Superkid Academy...faced her with the love of God.

Yet in these thoughts myself almost despising,
Haply I think on thee, and then my state,
Like to the lark at break of day arising

From sullen earth, sings hymns at heaven's gate;
For thy sweet love remember'd such wealth brings
That then I scorn to change my state with kings.

And then, after a pause, she closed with, "Thank you."

The crowd clapped, though sporadically, as if unsure if they should break the solemn moment.

Mashela walked off the stage. Missy jumped back into the shadows as Mashela skirted by, not even seeing her. As Missy watched her walk through the corridor and turn the corner, her heart felt saddened for her. She was so talented, so intelligent…and so alone.

As the next girl walked out onstage, Missy retreated to the ready area. She sat at her vanity table, practicing her scales again, looking at nothing in the distance. Her voice was fine, but her thoughts bent toward Mashela. She had caused Missy so much trouble. She had run her through the wringer. And the pageant wasn't over—there was probably more to come. Missy braced herself. Yet she realized that Mashela, despite her strength on the outside, was as lost as ever on the inside. She had no friends, no connection to her parents, no hope for her future. A lump rose in Missy's throat. In some ways she hoped Mashela would win the contest—maybe it would be a highlight in her life.

Missy performed her song perfectly, her voice flowing smoothly and clearly. The music was played at just the right volume and she received a standing ovation. For a moment, she thought she saw Mashela watching her, glaring at her. The competition between them was certainly close. If either of them had a chance at winning, the other was surely runner-up. But only time would tell.

▲　▲　▲

Diamond Earrings entered the ready room. "Girls! Girls! May I have your attention?"

The room quieted down.

"The judges have narrowed the competition down to just 10 girls. It's been a close and a tough decision, but they're ready to get one step closer to selecting this year's Miss Nautical Christmas. Does everyone have on their final evening outfits? Good. Line up here, in numerical order, please."

Each girl took the place she'd had at the beginning of the competition. This was one of the hardest parts of the contest. Everyone would be standing onstage, but only 10 would be picked to continue. It was gut-wrenching just waiting—and hoping—for your name. And for those who weren't picked, it was heartbreaking—and especially difficult to keep a smile on your face while others were picked instead of you.

The girls filed onto the stage, taking their place on stair-step bleachers. Every one of them could be seen by all. The lights were too bright to see the audience, but Missy knew her mother, father, Paul, Rapper and his dad were out there. She wished Valerie, her best friend and roommate at Superkid Academy, could be here too. Valerie never put too much stock in outward beauty, but she would be cheering Missy along with the rest of them.

"And our 10 finalists are…"

One by one, Diamond Earrings called out names. Each time, the audience roared and the winner seemed completely surprised. When picked, she would walk down through all the other smiling girls and make her way to centerstage.

When Diamond Earrings was down to number four, Missy felt a twinge of concern. She *had* to at least make the final 10. Sure, she almost took out a judge with the heel of her shoe, but who could count that against her? After all, she *was* completely adorable in her Santa outfit—and her song went very well. Missy endured.

"Natasha Wong," Diamond Earrings announced. A cute girl of Asian descent screamed and made her way to the front.

Only three more, Missy thought.

"Stephanie Enrad." Stephanie—four girls away from Missy—made her way down front.

"Mashela Knavery." Missy's mouth nearly dropped. *Mashela got called before me?* Mashela flashed a big smile and squeezed the hand of the girl next to her. She went down to the front and stood amid the lights and camera flashes.

Please, oh, please, oh, please!

"Missy Ashton," Diamond Earrings announced. Missy screamed. She didn't mean to, but she did. The knot in her stomach immediately disappeared and she felt like she was watching from afar.

Missy smiled wide and made her way through the other girls, just imagining what their thoughts were toward her, the girl who had bodyguards.

She took her place at the end of the line, beside Mashela.

The crowd cheered, the girls smiled and waved, the curtains closed.

Mashela turned to Missy. "Good luck," she said.

"I don't believe in luck," Missy responded quickly.

"You should," Mashela returned. "It got you *this* far."

Diamond Earrings walked over. "OK, girls, well done. Now listen—I need you to stand over here." She waltzed them to the side, just offstage behind the curtain. "Stand

here until I call your name. Then come to centerstage. I'll
ask you a question and you'll give an answer in one minute
or less. Your final placement is based largely upon the
quality of your answer. Understand?"

The girls nodded.

"Good. We'll start in just a moment."

Diamond Earrings walked off. Missy looked at the other
girls. Every one of them seemed a bit nervous. One was
twisting a lock of her hair. Another was squeezing her hands.
Missy was rocking on her heel until she remembered what
had happened the last time she'd done that. Mashela seemed
surprisingly cool. But Missy knew she could put on a
show—and she may have been doing just that.

"I heard your poem," Missy whispered to her.

Mashela suddenly flipped her head toward
Missy. "What?"

"I heard your poem. It was pretty."

Mashela huffed. "It was a sonnet."

"Well, whatever it was, I liked it. I didn't know you
read Shakespeare."

"I'm just full of surprises. Get a clue, Ashton. I was
playing the audience. I don't even know what that thing
even said." She turned away and stared toward the stage.
Her glare was hollow.

Missy just nodded. It didn't matter. Soon this silly competition would be over and, hopefully, Mashela would give up.

Moments later, the first of the 10 was called out onstage to answer a question. She approached Diamond Earrings and smiled. Her stage presence was good.

Diamond said, "You've told us you want to help fix society's flaws. What do you believe is society's greatest flaw?"

The girl paused and looked down. She wasn't ready for it. Missy knew that was one of the easiest mistakes to make: writing a blanket statement like that on your questionnaire, but then not having specific examples to back it up. The girl finally responded, listing several things she didn't like, but her answers came off more critical than hopeful. Next!

Number two seemed nervous, Missy thought, *and it showed.* The girl must have said on her questionnaire that she was some sort of climber, because her question was: What is the hardest place to climb and what would it take to get you to climb it?

It wasn't necessarily a hard question, Missy thought. *If she were the contestant, she'd turn the question around to be a metaphor. Say, for instance, that the hardest place to climb is to one's full potential. Something like that. Talk*

about the barriers of your doubt and how faith can get you
beyond the highest walls. Yeah, that sounded good.

But the girl completely flubbed. Missy was right, she
was nervous. She just named some mountain and said she
didn't ever want to climb it again. Not exactly the answer
the judges were looking for. Next!

One by one, the girls answered difficult questions, some
answering better than others. But no one yet did a "stand-
out" job. At a young age, Missy had been professionally
trained in this area—and it was easy for her to see what
needed to be adjusted each time. In terms of competition,
Missy was feeling pretty good so far.

"Mashela Knavery."

Oh, here we go, Missy thought.

Mashela walked forward and took her place onstage.
She looked fabulous in her deep crimson evening gown
with her hair pulled up. Her eyes twinkled and her teeth
shined. Missy let out a long, slow breath.

Diamond Earrings smiled and said, "Mashela, the judges
have asked that we ask you a question not related to your
questionnaire. You mentioned before reading your sonnet
that you don't know your parents well. So we want to know
who do you look up to the most, and why?"

Missy raised her eyebrows. That was a good question.

Missy had no clue what Mashela would say. General Fear? Major Dread? Not exactly the cornerstones of society…

Mashela didn't lose a beat. "Oh, most definitely, the person I look up to the most is my best friend, Tootle."

Missy suddenly choked. She started coughing and stepped away from the other girls. She was thumping her chest, trying to regain control.

She heard Mashela continue, "Tootle is the kind of friend that…she's always there for you. Believing the best of you. For instance, there was the time when I was on top of a building, near the edge both physically and emotionally. And, Tootle"—Mashela paused—"she grabbed my hand and said, 'God loves you. You're not alone. We're the same.'"

Missy finally stopped coughing. She tried to keep her eyes from watering and ruining her makeup.

"Ever since then, my goal has been to reach out to others the way she reached out to me. To grab others from the edge and let them know they're not alone. That God loves them and we're all the same."

Mashela patted the corners of her eyes with her fingertips.

Diamond Earrings thanked her for her answer and Mashela left the stage. As she passed, Missy cleared her throat and said, "You're quite the politician."

Mashela smiled. "That was actually fun."

From stage: "And our final contestant is Missy Ashton."

Missy put on a glamorous smile, straightened her dress and walked onstage. She wore an off-white dress this time and her hair was up, too. She played to the lights and the cameras, putting into practice all the little tips she gathered from previous contests.

Missy stopped beside Diamond Earrings, who greeted her. Then she said, "Missy, the question our judges have for you is this: What has been your most difficult challenge in readjusting to society?"

Missy looked at Diamond Earrings and after a moment's thought, she said, "I'm sorry. I don't think I understand the question."

*Great. That was going to cost her some points. But better **that** than answer incorrectly.*

Diamond Earrings said, "Well, you stated on your questionnaire that you were raised by wolves until your parents found you. What was the biggest challenge you faced when you left the wilderness and re-entered society?"

Missy blinked.

The auditorium was silent.

She blinked again.

Her stomach felt empty.

Her vision blurred.

She stole a glance at the side stage area and saw Mashela blow a kiss, wink and walk away. Missy didn't know how, but somehow that girl had tampered with her questionnaire.

Missy shook it off. She cleared her head and prayed to God. *Father, let Your words fill my mouth. I need Your strength. I need Your wisdom. And...I forgive Mashela. I won't hate her. I won't. If I need to give this competition to her, I will. But I want Your will, not mine.*

Missy felt her mouth moving and she hoped she was saying the right thing.

"It's difficult to adjust to society," Missy said, her voice growing stronger. "When you feel like an outcast, it's sometimes easier to act like...like a wolf...than the person you were created to be."

Missy swallowed hard. "Sometimes, if a wolf is hurt and you try to help, it doesn't understand. It will growl and threaten you and maybe even hurt you—and all you were trying to do was help it. I can't say I know why. But I've discovered that some people are that way, too. You want to help them. You try to help them. But no matter what you do, they fight you every step of the way. They lash out at you and provoke you. And there's no clear reason, except you know they must be hurting. That's why the best response—the only appropriate response—is love."

Missy turned to Diamond Earrings. "On that questionnaire, there was a question about what you would take to heaven if you had to go today. Well, I believe in heaven, and when I go, the one thing I want to take with me is the assurance that I helped the wolves of society in the best way I knew how."

Missy shrugged. "Who knows. Maybe I'll never fit in completely. But I do know what has been the biggest challenge for me: And that is, reaching out in love—even to those who don't deserve it."

Missy smiled again and then slightly stepped back. She thought she'd rambled a little bit, but it wasn't bad. The audience stayed completely silent. Diamond Earrings was waiting for the applause, but it didn't come. She motioned for Missy to go ahead and take her place backstage and Missy walked off.

When she reached the side, Paul was there. "Good save!" he whispered.

"Where's Mashela?"

"She just stormed off. I think it really made her mad that you recovered so well."

"I just spoke from my heart," Missy said softly. She

looked out onstage again, remembering that she was in a competition. Diamond Earrings was making some final announcements.

"They didn't clap," Missy said to Paul. "What does that mean?"

"I don't know," Paul replied. "But we're about to find out."

One hundred girls stood onstage wondering who would be picked. The 10 girls in the front row were especially curious, Missy being one of them. The audience applauded a trio of horn players who blew out "Jingle Bell Rock." As the trio left the stage, Diamond Earrings took their place. She was smiling ear to ear, pleased to be the one with the "big announcement."

She pulled out a series of red and green envelopes and waved them with her left hand. She announced that she had the judges' final decisions in hand.

The audience clapped again and Diamond Earrings ripped open the first envelope.

"And the second runner-up is…" She held the paper up to the light. "Natasha Wong!"

Natasha burst into tears and walked up to the front of the stage. She thanked Diamond and the audience.

Diamond Earrings lifted the second envelope. She tore it open. She said, "And the first runner-up is… Mashela Knavery!"

Mashela immediately looked at Missy. She looked

confused. She was obviously weighing the same questions Missy was: *Does this mean she'd actually knocked Missy out of the competition? Or...does it mean she came in second place to her rival?*

Mashela walked to the front, tight-jawed. She nodded to Diamond and the audience. Not exactly the response everyone was expecting. But Missy knew the truth. She knew Mashela wouldn't be satisfied until she knew if she had robbed Missy of the title.

Missy held her breath and closed her eyes.

Diamond Earrings lifted the final envelope.

She held it up, and tore it open.

She removed the paper and said, "And the *winner* of tonight's Miss Nautical Christmas Pageant is..."

Missy squeezed her hands together.

The audience was silent.

Just as Missy opened her eyes, she heard her name: "Missy Ashton!"

The audience exploded in cheers. They stood and applauded.

Missy felt a rush of heat flow over her body—a mix of surprise and relief and excitement.

She walked across the stage, feeling as though she was walking on air. She completely ignored any scowls behind her. She knew half the girls were thinking her dad probably *did* bribe the judges. But it didn't matter. One day they would see the truth.

Humbly, Missy accepted the crown from Diamond Earrings. She bent down as the sparkling circlet was placed on her head. A tall man in a black tuxedo handed her a bouquet of a dozen red roses. Their fragrance filled the stage.

The lights shimmered, the audience thundered. Missy said "thank you" at least 20 times. She felt a soft tear running down her face. She'd done it—despite all the persecution Mashela had provided. *She'd done it!*

Missy squinted and she saw her parents in the front, with Paul and Rapper. Her mother was exclaiming, "That's my daughter!" Her father was clapping vigorously. Paul and Rapper were hooting and hollering. Mr. Rapfield, Rapper's dad, was standing and applauding, too.

"Ugh!"

Missy yelped as the roses were jerked out of her hands. Mashela grabbed them with full force and pushed Missy back. Missy caught herself, but not before she knocked Runner-Up #2 to the ground. Diamond Earrings shrieked and grabbed Mashela by the arm. Mashela, of course, quickly shook her off. Black Tuxedo ran back onstage and grabbed Mashela's arms from behind. The roses went flying.

"Let go!" she cried as she kicked back, hitting his shin and sending him to the ground. Paul and Rapper leapt onstage, coming to Missy's aid. Mashela spun and reached for Missy's crown. She had just about grabbed it when Paul and Rapper yanked Missy backward. At the same time, Geek and Eek appeared out of nowhere and locked Mashela's hands behind her back with a pair of electronic handcuffs. Mashela flipped and kicked Eek in the stomach, throwing him to the ground. The 97 contestants standing on the bleachers were screaming, not quite sure what to do.

"Stop it!" Missy cried. "Stop it!"

Paul and Rapper dodged a quick blow and grabbed Mashela's ankles. She fell onto her backside, pinning her cuffs in the small of her back. She cried out in anger and pain.

Missy grabbed Diamond's slender microphone and shouted, "Stop it! *Stop it!*"

Immediately everyone froze.

The auditorium fell silent.

Missy felt suddenly awkward. She softly addressed the audience. "I'm...I'm sorry. I'm sorry to involve all of you. This is...it's between me and Mashela."

Whispers wove through the crowd. Missy picked up the roses and shuffled them together. Mashela looked so angry,

bound in handcuffs…and hate. Missy looked at the roses
again. She looked behind Mashela at all the girls standing
there, staring at her, wondering what she was going to do
next. She knew half of them were just waiting for her to
prove the rumors right.

Missy prayed one word: "Wisdom." And the Lord
responded with one word: *Love.*

Looking into Mashela's eyes, Missy peered past the
piercing anger. She caught a glimpse of the sadness
there…the sadness that had been there since the day they
had met.

Missy turned to the audience. "There's…something you
should know."

Mashela glared at her.

Paul and Rapper, still holding Mashela's ankles, looked
at each other in wonderment.

"My nickname," Missy announced, "is *Tootle.*"

Murmurs filled the auditorium.

Diamond Earrings came forward. "Wait a *second—
you're* Tootle?" She pointed at Mashela. "She said you were
her *best friend.*"

Missy nodded. "Well, we've had our differences, but
some of what she said was true. You see, in many ways
we're the same. And that's why I…I believe she deserves

to win this competition as much as I do."

Diamond Earrings' mouth dropped. "I don't think so. Believe me when I say she has been disqualified."

"No." Missy took off her crown. "I'm going to take the blame for this. It's my fault. I should be disqualified." Missy nodded at Paul and Rapper. "Go ahead, let her go."

Diamond Earrings couldn't believe it. "Are you saying you started this?"

"I'm ending it," Missy stated. She motioned to Geek, since Eek still wasn't standing. "Please uncuff her." He looked at Mr. Ashton, who nodded. Geek obeyed.

Mashela, entirely disarmed, stood up slowly, unsure. Missy handed her the bouquet. Confused, Mashela accepted it. Then Missy looked at the beautiful crown. She placed it on Mashela's head.

"What are you doing?!" Mashela demanded through clenched teeth.

"I'm giving up my place," Missy whispered. "That means you came in first." Then to the audience, Missy announced, "Miss Nautical Christmas—Mashela Knavery!"

"That's my daughter!" Mr. Ashton shouted. And the auditorium erupted in cheers.

Missy put her arm around Mashela, who stood there completely stunned.

"Smile," Missy said to her. "This is your night."

Mashela smiled weakly as she said, "This *isn't* my night. And this *isn't* over."

"I know," Missy said with a grin. "Now smile before you spoil the moment."

Pop! Pop! Pop! Pop! More flashes exploded as people shouted.

Moments later, the music started again and they were pushed offstage. As they went, Missy heard girls wishing her well and saying what a good friend she was. They hadn't believed those rumors for a moment. Missy thanked them for the compliments. Diamond Earrings even caught her before she left and congratulated her on being such a good person: "You've come so far since being in the wolf pack!"

Missy just nodded. Before she knew it, Mashela was gone.

▲ ▲ ▲

After collecting Missy's things and talking to some reporters, Missy's dad ushered them into a hoverlimo he had waiting. They got inside and took off, heading to the Christmas Angel dinner. Rapper joined his dad in his rental hovercar.

Missy looked out the limo's window as they pulled

away. "I think that'll be my last pageant for a while," she said.

Paul said, "Are you kidding? Things got topsy-turvy and you *still* won. You oughta make this a career."

Missy grimaced. "No thank you," she said. "Some girls are made for this, but I need something a little less nerve-racking."

"Here, here," Mr. Ashton chimed in.

"So," Paul said, "you think that'll be the last we hear from Mashela? She got what she wanted—your crown."

"But only because I gave it to her," Missy corrected. "What she really wanted was me to stop loving her, and that hasn't happened."

"You think she'll try to do something else?" Mrs. Ashton asked with concern.

"Well, it's not Christmas yet," Missy said. "I'm sure she's still scheming to steal it."

Paul asked, "So when does this cat and mouse game stop?"

Missy let her hair down and shook her head. "It stops when I quit loving Mashela, or she quits hating me. And I don't think I helped things by giving the pageant to her. She was pretty steamed. But I'm not giving in to the pressure. Acts 20:24 says I shouldn't let things like this move me. If I stay strong, I'll keep my joy."

"So what are you going to do?" Paul asked.

Missy didn't know the answer. She sat back and the car grew quiet. She watched the scenery roll by. It wasn't entirely clear-cut to her. But it *was* clear-cut to Someone. Missy closed her eyes and prayed silently.

Father God, You've honored me and given me wisdom tonight on how to restore my honor. You have come through time and again for me when I'm dealing with Mashela. Now I need Your wisdom one more time. I need to know how to end this. What can I do to keep her from hating me so much? Or is that a decision she has to make?

Missy opened her eyes and watched the snow-covered trees go by. They stopped for a moment and she saw a squirrel's footprints in the snowdrifts. Multicolored Christmas lights twinkled from storefronts. Icicles hung from up high. It was so pretty. It was Christmas. Maybe it wasn't Christmas Day yet, but Christmas *was* here—in her heart.

Suddenly, the Holy Spirit recalled Romans 12:21 to Missy's memory: *Do not be overcome by evil, but overcome evil with good.*

You already know what to do, He said boldly to Missy. The Superkid examined her heart. Yes, she already *knew* what to do.

"Daddy, can we swing by home before we go to the dinner?"

Mr. Ashton looked at his daughter, sitting across from him. "It's OK," he said. "We have three guards at the house. And Killer's there."

Mrs. Ashton looked at him.

He shrugged. "Well, the three guards will keep it safe anyway."

"I know," Missy said, "but I really need to stop by home."

Mr. Ashton looked into his daughter's blue eyes for a long moment and then turned. To the driver, he said, "Let's detour to the house before we go to the gala."

The driver said, "Yes sir," and turned around at the next intersection.

▲   ▲   ▲

In the circular driveway in front of her house, Missy jumped out of the hoverlimo and told them she'd return in a few minutes. She ran up the front sidewalk and spoke to the guard. He let her in the house.

Ten minutes later she exited and gave a handful of items to the guard. She gave him specific instructions. He looked at his watch and nodded.

Missy returned to the hoverlimo and said it was all right to go to the dinner now. Mr. and Mrs. Ashton and Paul looked at her with curiosity. She smiled at them.

"Just applying the last bit of pressure," she said.

Mashela thought it was a little odd there were no guards at the Ashton household when she arrived. But then again, the Ashtons were a little odd, so why think anything of it?

After leaving the pageant in a rage, she'd caught up with them at the Christmas Angel Dinner Thingy that, Mashela thought, was more about hype than doing anyone any good. Then again, Mashela didn't really care. At least it was a distraction for Missy and her family. It gave Mashela time for the final attempt she needed to steal Missy's Christmas.

If Missy ever deserved to have her Christmas ruined, she did now. Who did she think she was, making a fool of Mashela in front of all those people? Mashela thought she'd acted so pompous. She'd given up her crown, given up her roses. She knew Missy didn't care about those things anyway. She had just wanted to *win* and then rub it in Mashela's face by giving them to her, reminding her that she was the *loser.*

And if that wasn't enough, she'd actually had the gall

to make it sound like she understood Shakespeare's sonnet. She could never understand it. Her life was too perfect. Well, Mashela was about to help her understand it more.

Mashela had brought all the right tools. In a flash, she removed a low, back window leading to the basement. She'd scoped out the dwelling long before and knew the basement was usually shut off to the rest of the house. It gave her time to prepare once she entered and—wouldn't you know it—the core of the alarm system was located there.

She put on a pair of infrared I-Glasses and could see like it was daylight. Carefully, but swiftly, she lowered herself into the basement. She slid down the wall, onto a long utility table. Next, she took on the security system, removing the main control panel. It was child's play. She had it rerouted in seconds. As far as the alarm company was concerned, the system was still on.

Mashela turned to a concrete wall with a heavy door and smiled. She approached a control pad on the wall and looked it over. This control pad opened the safe, where all the Ashton's Christmas presents were stored…for now. Mashela dug into her small backpack and found the device she needed. She removed the control pad cover and attached the device to three wire connections. A digital display scrolled a series of red numbers until the match was found.

Pop! She heard the safe door release. It was almost too easy. These high-dollar executive-types always buy the latest and greatest safes…which always have the latest and greatest flaws. With thin gloves on her hands, she pulled the door open.

Her eyes twinkled in excitement. In her mind, she was already composing the note she'd leave in the safe. Something like, *Sorry, Santa went to the Bahamas this year. No yum-yums for you!* Or then again, maybe something simple would be better. Like, *Nothing personal.*

When the door opened, Mashela's mouth dropped. From wall to wall, the large safe was empty. Completely empty.

Then she chuckled. *Did the Ashtons actually think that because the pageant was over, she would disappear? Did they put all their presents out already?* Mashela shook her head. They were *so* naïve. *This* she would have to see. She closed the safe door and left the area as she'd found it. She left the tiny escape window open for a quick getaway.

Mashela walked up the stairs and quietly opened the door leading into the house.

Killer came around the corner and started growling. She quickly removed her I-Glasses. When the dog recognized her, he got excited and started wagging his tail. She petted him and whispered, "Hey, boy. You like that steak I gave you?" She reached into her backpack and removed a pack of hot dogs. She pulled three out and tossed them down the hall. Killer went charging after them, thrilled to be playing a new game. Mashela walked toward the living room, staying in the shadows. Up ahead, she saw the room was bright and twinkling, grotesquely pushing the Christmas spirit on all who entered.

She glanced in and saw the most beautiful Christmas holo-tree. She paused and looked at it a moment. Underneath it were mounds of presents, begging to be opened. The Ashtons wouldn't know what hit them. She walked past the room and checked the entryway. When she saw it was empty, she checked the kitchen, dining room and stairway, too. If anyone was in the house, they were upstairs and she'd hear them before they were close enough to catch her. She returned to the living room.

Taking in the scene took her breath away. The evergreen Christmas tree was highlighted with twinkling white lights and golden ribbon. Underneath, the presents matched perfectly. Stepping into the room felt like she was stepping onto holy ground. She pushed forward, but caught herself. It *wasn't* holy ground. It was just Missy's house—full of more good things than the Superkid deserved.

Mashela stepped forward, devising plans about how she could utterly destroy Missy's Christmas once and for all. Yes, then Missy would learn love isn't as strong as she thought. She would learn that life held as much loss as it did joy...maybe more. She would prove Missy's love could fail.

Standing in front of the tree, Mashela bent down and grabbed the nearest present. She wondered: Should she open it, break it or absolutely mutilate it? She flipped it over, ready to tear into it.

And she dropped it.

And she stared at it.

Written across the gift tag were the words:

To: Mashela
From: Missy

Was this some sort of trick? Mashela pulled out a switchblade and spun around. No one was there. Why did she feel like she wasn't alone? Something was wrong with this. Very wrong. She retracted the knife.

Slowly she bent down and flipped over the tag of another present. It said:

To: Mashela
From: Missy

And another:

To: Mashela
From: Missy

And another:

To: Mashela
From: Missy

What was Missy trying to prove? Mashela wondered.
Why is she—

Mashela lifted up a present in the center of the pack.

Click! Mashela leapt back and swiftly drew her
switchblade again. Ready for a fight, she quickly scanned
the room. Suddenly, the beautiful holo-tree disappeared
and a hologram of Missy took its place. She was wearing
the same off-white dress Mashela had last seen her in.
Her hair was down, though…and she was looking straight
at her.

Missy said, "Surprise!"

Mashela stood her ground.

Missy's hologram continued. "Sorry I didn't have time to change into a Santa uniform like you did, but my time's short." She looked to the side, then back at Mashela. "I realized something tonight. I'm not sure when. Maybe it was when I won. Maybe it was on the way home. I don't know, maybe I've always known it. I realized that I was being selfish, and I'm sorry."

Mashela couldn't take her eyes off Missy. Of course she was selfish…but…she admits it?

"I realized that ever since I was born, I've won Christmas pageants. I've eaten Christmas cookies. I've hung Christmas lights. I've packed snow into Christmas snowmen. I've had Christmas every year. But you…I don't know if you've ever had a real Christmas. So now, with no crowds around, no witnesses, just you and me, I want to *give* you Christmas."

Missy leaned forward. "I know you wanted to steal it. But you can't. I'm *giving* it to you. These were all my presents and, whatever they are, I give them to you."

Mashela looked behind herself again. Killer walked into the room and sat down.

"It's no trick. There're no guards, no surprises. Well,

there's a dog, but...I don't think you'll have a problem with that."

Killer's head popped up. He whimpered, then lay down.

"Truth is, Mashela, you almost did it. You *almost* stole my Christmas. All along you had me wondering: Who will win? You or me? Cat or mouse? But you know what? Life isn't a cartoon. Neither of us can paint a black hole on a wall and escape our problems. We have to face them head on. And, see, that's where it's so good to be a Christian. Because where my love runs out, God's love takes over. So go ahead—keep this competition up as long as you want. Fight me, hurt me, steal from me. Every time you do, I'm just going to love you more—in Jesus' Name."

Mashela stood there, not sure what to do...what to think.

"Do you even know what Christmas is about? It's about celebrating the fact that God loves you so much, He sent His only Son Jesus to earth. Jesus came and died for all the bad things you've done—all of them. He took your punishment...your place. Then He rose from the grave, defeating death itself.

"So, Mashela, Christmas means those bad things you've done don't matter anymore. Christmas means if you ask Him, God can change you. I mean, look at me. Without Jesus, I'm as vain and selfish as they come. But *with*

Him…I have the strength to give my worst enemy one of my greatest loves."

Missy looked to the side again as she said, "Anyway, I have to go. My parents are waiting." Then after a long pause, she said, "Merry Christmas, Mashela. Merry Christmas." And then she disappeared. The sparkling tree reappeared and Mashela was left staring at it. She felt emotion from deep inside welling up within her.

Shaking it off, she spun around and tightened her jaw. Her fingers brushed the Nativity scene, and she stopped. She couldn't take her eyes off it. The marble Nativity set had cows and lambs and goats, wise men, shepherds and Mary and Joseph. And there…in the center…was Baby Jesus. With a shaking hand, Mashela reached out and picked Him up.

He was so small…and so fragile. God's Son, sent into the world. He could have sent a ruler, a king, a commander. But He sent a *baby*.

A warm tear crawled down Mashela's cheek. She felt a peace wrap around her like she'd never felt before. She crumpled to the ground and began to cry. Deep, heavy sobs rolled from inside her. The Jesus figurine in her hand pressed back, as she squeezed it as hard as she could.

Christmas morning was exhilarating. Missy'd had a good night's sleep once she let everything with Mashela go. She was a bit surprised to return after the dinner to find Mashela hadn't even been there, as far as she could tell. Nothing was out of order. *Maybe,* Missy thought, *Mashela finally did give up.* In a week, Missy would be back at Superkid Academy and they could follow up on things. But meanwhile, her Christmas was *here* and it was heart-lifting. Although it had been a bit awkward, having to explain to everyone why the presents were out of the safe and hers were under the tree labeled, *To: Mashela.*

Missy, her parents and Paul arose early and gathered in the living room to open presents. As they opened them, they drank hot chocolate and laughed. For the first time in a while, Missy felt completely safe.

The ComPhone rang and Mr. Ashton dashed to the kitchen to get it. He brought it into the living room so everyone could join in the call. Rapper was on the line.

"Hey guys!" he said through the screen. The family

greeted him. Then he said, "Check it out!"

Rapper held the morning newspaper up to the screen. On the front page was a big picture of Missy smiling and placing her crown on Mashela's head. The headline read: "Wolf-Girl Gives Crown to Runner-Up."

"Ugh!" Missy shouted playfully. "Leave it to reporters to not check their facts!"

"Yeah," Paul said. "They should have said '*First* Runner-Up.'"

Missy thumped his leg with her fist. "I mean about me being raised by wolves."

Paul laughed, holding his leg.

Rapper said things were great at his dad's. They'd arrived home in the early morning and just decided to celebrate Christmas then. He was exhausted and was ready for sleep. The Ashtons laughed and said goodbye.

After they hung up, Paul said, "I was just thinking of something. How did Mr. Rapfield know to come to the auditorium to find Rapper?"

Missy looked at Paul. That was a good question. She looked at her parents. They just smiled.

"Wait," Paul said. "Did you guys have something to do with his dad coming?"

Mr. and Mrs. Ashton didn't say a word.

Missy nodded with a big grin. "Daddy's got connections."

The DobShepPoo bounded in the room. "C'mere, Hot Dog!" Missy shouted.

Paul dropped his head and looked at Missy disbelieving. "You named him *Hot Dog?*"

"Yeah," Missy said, scratching behind the dog's ears. "I realized when we came in last night that he kinda smells like hot dogs, so…"

Paul put his nose on the dog's back and sniffed. "He doesn't smell like hot dogs!"

"Well, he did last night."

"It's not a very scary name."

"Sure it is! If I were a burglar and I saw a hot dog as big as this dog coming at me, I'd run."

Paul laughed. "OK, I'll give you that one."

The next hour or so was spent laughing and telling stories. Missy's dad had a hundred of them. Shortly after, they cleaned up the room, throwing away torn gift wrap. Missy looked at the pile of presents at her side and realized how blessed she was to have Christmases like this. Paul looked equally thankful. Missy only wished Mashela could have had some of the presents. She really wanted her to have *something* this year…even after everything she had done.

Then Mrs. Ashton spotted something under the tree, in

the far corner. She bent down and reached back to retrieve it. She looked at the tag and read:

To: Missy
From: Santa

Missy looked up. She looked at Paul. She looked at her dad, then her mom. Her mother gave her the tiny gift. It fit in the palm of her hand. "OK, which of you is this from?" she asked.

Missy looked at each of them again, but they all seemed as interested as she was to see what was inside. Around the middle was a thin, golden ribbon. Missy pulled it and it lay over the sides of her open hand. She put the gift in her lap and tore open the paper. Inside was a little, black, velvet case. Missy lifted open its hinged cover and gasped. Inside, shiny as ever, was the simple, silver friendship ring Paul had given her months ago.

"It's…your ring…" Paul said curiously.

Missy's eyes teared up as she pulled it out of the box and slid it on her finger. It fit perfectly.

A tear dropped to the ground. Now everything was perfect. *Everything.* Missy couldn't decide which she was happier about: getting her ring back, or realizing that maybe

Mashela did get a gift this Christmas, after all.

Her gaze immediately shot to the marble Nativity scene and she noticed for the first time that the Baby Jesus she'd put out the night before was missing. And Missy began to cry. Not from sadness, but from joy—because Jesus was no longer in the manger. He was in their hearts and in their lives. And because of Him, Missy had a love in her heart so strong that nothing, and no one, could *ever* take it away.

The End

Prayer for Salvation

Father God, I believe that Jesus is Your Son and that You raised Him from the dead for me. Jesus, I give my life to You. Right now, I make You the Lord of my life and choose to follow You forever. I love You and I know You love me. Thank You, Jesus, for giving me a new life. Thank You for coming into my heart and being my Savior. I am a child of God! Amen.

About the Author

For more than 15 years, Christopher Maselli has been sharing God's Word with kids through fiction. With a Master of Fine Arts in Writing, he is the author of more than 50 books, including the *Super Sleuth Investigators* mysteries, the *Amazing Laptop* series and the *Superkids Adventures.*

Chris lives in Fort Worth, Texas, with his wife and three children. His hobbies include running, collecting *"It's a Wonderful Life"* movie memorabilia and "way too much" computing.

Visit his website at ChristopherPNMaselli.com.

Other Products Available

Products Designed for Today's Children and Youth

And Jesus Healed Them All (confession book and CD gift package)
Baby Praise Board Book
Baby Praise Christmas Board Book
Load Up—A Youth Devotional
Over the Edge—A Youth Devotional
The Best of *Shout!* Adventure Comics
The *Shout!* Joke Book
The *Shout!* Super-Activity Book
Wichita Slim's Campfire Stories

Commander Kellie and the Superkids™ Books:

Superkid Academy Children's Church Curriculum (DVD/CD curriculum)
* • Volume 1—My Father Loves Me!
* • Volume 2—The Fruit of the Spirit in You
* • Volume 3—The Sweet Life
* • Volume 4—Living in THE BLESSING
    • Volume 5—The Superkid Creed

The SWORD Adventure Book
Commander Kellie and the Superkids™
    Solve-It-Yourself Mysteries
Commander Kellie and the Superkids™ Adventure Series:
Middle Grade Novels by Christopher P.N. Maselli:

#1 The Mysterious Presence
#2 The Quest for the Second Half
#3 Escape From Jungle Island
#4 In Pursuit of the Enemy
#5 Caged Rivalry
#6 Mystery of the Missing Junk
#7 Out of Breath
#8 The Year Mashela Stole Christmas
#9 False Identity
#10 The Runaway Mission
#11 The Knight-Time Rescue of Commander Kellie

*Available in Spanish

We're Here for You!®

Your growth in God's WORD and victory in Jesus are at the very center of our hearts. In every way God has equipped us, we will help you deal with the issues facing you, so you can be the **victorious overcomer** He has planned for you to be.

The mission of Kenneth Copeland Ministries is about all of us growing and going together. Our prayer is that you will take full advantage of all The WORD has given us to share with you.

Wherever you are in the world, you can watch the *Believer's Voice of Victory* broadcast on television (check your local listings), the Internet at kcm.org or on our digital Roku channel.

Our website, **kcm.org,** gives you access to every resource we've developed for your victory. And, you can find contact information for our international offices in Africa, Asia, Australia, Canada, Europe, Ukraine and our headquarters in the United States.

Each office is staffed with devoted men and women, ready to serve and pray with you. You can contact the worldwide office nearest you for assistance, and you can call us for prayer at our U.S. number, +1-817-852-6000, 24 hours every day!

We encourage you to connect with us often and let us be part of your everyday walk of faith!

Jesus Is LORD!

Kenneth & Gloria Copeland

Kenneth and Gloria Copeland

9 781575 626598